ZERO CITY

Geonn Cannon

Supposed Crimes LLC • Matthews, North Carolina

www.supposedcrimes.com

This book is typeset in Goudy Old Style.

ZERO CITY

PROLOGUE

ELISE HERALD woke up in a strange bed. She was used to country sounds, horses and maybe a crop duster buzzing a nearby field. Mornings in Manhattan were a completely different thing.

After spending a few minutes hugging her pillow, listening to voices in the hallway and neighboring apartments, she got up and dragged herself into the shower. She hoped today would be a hot water day, and she was disappointed. In the kitchen, still wrapped in her towel, she was again disappointed to discover that she was out of oatmeal. She settled for toast - dry, since she had also run out of butter - and opened the newspaper to the want ads. There was a defeated slump to her shoulders as she scanned the page, already certain it would be a waste of time. She'd already gone through most of the available mechanic listings, all of whom had turned cold when they found out she was a woman.

Her mood perked up when she spotted a new listing. Achilles Cab Company. They were looking for a mechanic, all shifts available, apply in person.

She circled it and headed out.

The company was located in a dingy garage just north of the Lincoln Tunnel, just close enough to the Hudson River to see the morning sunlight sparkle on its water between the trees. She took the subway and walked the rest of the way, trying to ignore how much the anonymous concrete buildings resembled a prison. She entered through a door marked with the company logo and found herself in a garage that only helped strengthen the prison analogy. Four men sat around a card table, two of them engaged in some kind of card game, while the third and fourth were arguing over something in the newspaper.

To her right, there was another chain-link enclosure around a small office. A man was locked inside, sitting at a desk and writing something. There was an intercom microphone by his right elbow, and his work space was surrounded by a precarious stack of binders and loose papers. The wall behind him had a half dozen keyrings hanging on pegs.

Elise went up to the gap in the cage where she assumed the drivers received their keys. The man at the desk was wearing dark sunglasses, despite the low lighting. He glanced up as she approached but didn't stop whatever he was writing. There was a nameplate on his desk that simply read MICK.

"Can I h-h-help you, miss?"

"I'm looking for work."

"We're full up on, uh, on drivers at the moment. But if you-you want to leave your contact info–"

"Not a driver," she said. "There was an ad in the paper. Mechanics?"

He looked up again, scanning her face as if there was a tell-tale sign of her automotive skills. "You know cars?"

She smiled and shrugged. "I know enough. I can troubleshoot, fix what needs fixing, swap out anything that's broken or worn-out. I can keep your cabs on the road. And if there are no problems to fix, I can pump gas, wash them, clean out the backseats, empty the ashtrays..."

Mick tapped his pen on the table. "Have you ever worked at a garage?"

"Not officially, no," she said. "But I've worked on a lot of cars in my life. I know what keeps them going. I know why they stop. And whatever problems I don't know, I can figure out fairly quick. My mother drives the same car she got in 1972, and she's never been to a real mechanic because I was always around to dig around inside it."

"Hm. Well." He looked past her. She turned to follow his gaze and saw a maintenance bay with three cabs inside. "We, well, we-we *do* need someone. A-a-a-and we can't really afford to be picky. Do you want to d-day shift or night?"

"What's the difference?"

"Days can be busy, but nights can get frantic," Mick said. "It's New York, you know, it's a crapshoot."

Elise chewed her bottom lip, unsure what to choose. "How about I work both and see which is the better fit? And that will give me a chance to show you how good I am. And you said you need the help."

"We're talking two twelve-hour shifts," he said. "You really think you can do a full day here?"

She thought about retracting the offer, but she knew she was about to convince him. "Sure. Just for the trial run. It'll be tough, but I'm dedicated."

Mick chuckled and sat up straighter. "Yeah, it sounds like it." He tapped the desk again, then dropped the pen and stood up. "Why not. Trial run. A-a-and you are *not* working both full shifts. Half and half, with time in between to go home and get some rest. Does that sound like a fair deal to you?"

She nodded enthusiastically. "Yes, definitely. That sounds more than fair."

"What's your name?"

"Elise Herald."

He nodded. "Nice to meet you, Elise Herald. There are lockers in there, and they have overalls inside. Find one that fits you." He pointed toward the maintenance bay. "Your t-t-trial by fire awaits."

"Thank you," she said.

She turned and crossed the garage. She had a job. Theoretically, at least, assuming she had a good first day. But she was confident that she would pass muster. She really had been the go-to for any kind of engine trouble her friends and family had, both personal vehicles and farm equipment. She doubted a bunch of cabs would present an issue.

She found the lockers, none of which were locked, and opened one. She found the white overalls, as promised, and took it out.

"Okay," she whispered to herself. "Here we go."

She was ready to start her new life. She hoped running away from the old one hadn't been a huge mistake.

There was only one way to find out.

CHAPTER ONE

SOMETIMES SALLY Rafferty saw the grid when she closed her eyes. The map of New York City was projected onto the back of her eyelids, numbers and cardinal directions, Broadway cutting through the center like a sash. Every intersection and every block ended up looking the same to her after a few years behind the wheel. The East River to the Hudson, swinging around the Battery, cutting through Central Park. She rarely had to go farther north than Harlem, but she went where the fare demanded.

Her twelve hour shift at the Achilles Cab Company started at four PM on weekdays, eight PM on weekends. It was a Thursday, so she arrived at a quarter to four and left her car in the lot next to the garage. It was a fenced-in lot with a dedicated entrance to the cab company, a security feature that kept them from being afraid of muggers waiting for them after a shift ended.

She walked down the sloped driveway to join the other cabbies waiting for the day shift to turn their cars in so they could take them back out. To her left was the dispatcher's cage, where Mick Makinet handed out their assignments. He shared the cramped space with the cashier William Ritz. They called Ritz "the Reverend" because he was meticulous with his count. He'd once driven five miles to a cabbie's home to return twenty cents he'd mistakenly overpaid.

Rafferty was halfway down the ramp when Doc Beeler, one of the other cabbies, shouted out to her. "Yo, Raff! You can go home! We already got our quota today!"

"The hell are you talking about, Doc?"

"We can only have one girl in the clubhouse at a time." Doc gestured toward the row of cabs. "Mick hired a new one this morning."

Rafferty followed his nod to a person in blue coveralls whose upper body was currently blocked by the open hood of Cab 921.

"Tell her I have seniority," Rafferty said, continuing on to Mick's cage. "I'm not going anywhere."

Mick was waiting for her at the window, holding out the sign-in sheet for her. Mick wasn't quite as trustworthy as the Reverend, but he was mostly honest and treated his drivers well. He was lanky and made of sharp angles, exuding the energy of a twitchy middle school science teacher. She'd never seen him without his signature pair of black sunglasses, even in the garage.

"Don't be so sure about, ah, who we'd choose if, if you... if you made it a choice," Mick stammered. The speech impediment didn't seem to be triggered by anything in particular, like stress or exhaustion, and Rafferty had gotten fairly good at tuning it out over the years. "You're a good driver, Raff, but, oh, we-we have a dozen drivers. I've been w-w-watching her since she got here this morning. She really knows her stuff, and she's quick, too. Mechanics like her are, well, they're worth keeping around."

"Are you calling me expendable, Mick?"

"I, I, well, I wouldn't... ah." He showed her his palms, then took back the sign-in sheet. "I'm just saying. You know. Fair warning before you make an enemy of her, hm?"

Rafferty took her trip sheets from him and went to wait for an assignment. The other drivers had a card table set up near the vending machines. They also had a cabinet game where they could play Frogger, but it cost a quarter and most drivers weren't willing to spend their hard-earned cash on it unless they were extremely desperate. The guys around the table were also night shift, and the closest thing to coworkers she had. She straddled the end of the bench and watched as they played through a few hands of Go Fish.

"Hi. Was it Raff...?"

Rafferty twisted to look behind her. The mechanic was standing there, smiling brightly. She was older than Rafferty expected. She was twenty-nine, and she guessed this new arrival was at least seven or eight years her senior. Her blonde hair was tied back, and she had a fringe of bangs across her forehead. She looked like a kindergarten teacher about to gather the students for an arts class. She smiled broadly, furthering the teacher comparison.

"Elise Herald." She held out her hand. "I overheard the guys tell you I was new."

"Rafferty." She gave Elise's hand a perfunctory squeeze so she'd put it down.

Elise's eyebrows lifted. "Your name is Rafferty? That's your whole name?"

The guys snickered. Rafferty tried to ignore them. "Sally. But no one calls me that."

"Oh. Okay. Well, I'll try to stay out of your way."

"I appreciate it." Rafferty turned back to the card game.

She didn't give Elise any more of her attention but, when Mick called her name a few minutes later, the mechanic had vanished. Rafferty retrieved the keys to Cab 582 and went to start her shift.

She had been driving for five years, and she was still sometimes surprised by the fact that someone always needed to go somewhere. She left the garage and had only been driving ten minutes before a man in a suit stepped off the curb and threw his hand in the air. She pulled to the curb and let him climb in the backseat. He brought a wave of cool autumn air with him. He grunted as he pulled the door shut behind him and said, "75 Rockefeller."

"You got it."

She caught his double-take in the rearview mirror when he realized his driver was a woman. She tried dressing to delay that realization as long as possible. Today she was in a T-shirt with her red hair tucked under a newsboy cap. It worked if passengers didn't bother giving her more than a passing glance, but those who did always felt the need to comment on it. They either heard her voice, looked at her for more than a second, or looked at the hack license she had displayed on the partition between the seats.

"Oh hey, a lady!"

"They have women drivers now?"

"Uh-oh, be sure to fasten your seatbelt, ha ha, I'm just kidding, sweetheart."

It was worth it for the women who visibly relaxed when they realized they hadn't just gotten into a car with a strange man. Most of them probably weren't even aware of the tension they let go.

Rafferty had seen it enough to recognize the release.

75 Rockefeller didn't react to her other than the initial look, for which she was grateful. She drove him to his destination, received her fare and a twenty cent tip, and continued on.

She picked up a couple who took five seconds out of their argument to say "Times Square," then spent the rest of the ride screaming at each other. The husband slipped money through the partition without breaking the rhythm of what he was saying, even though his wife was already out of the cab and storming down the sidewalk. He gave chase, and Rafferty moved on.

A crying teenager with dark black eyeshadow and piles of cotton candy blonde hair asked if she knew "the place where Nancy died." Rafferty clarified that the girl meant Sid Vicious' girlfriend Nancy Spungen and took her to the Chelsea Hotel, where she left the girl sobbing on the sidewalk. She was surprised to discover there were groupies for groupies, but she supposed every famous person had fans somewhere.

Three Spanish tourists wanted to see the Statue of Liberty, so she took them to the Battery. After she dropped them off, she picked up a German couple who had already seen the tourist trap and took them to Katz's Deli. A customer got into her cab before the door could close and sent her to NYU. She was grateful that trip was short, because the smell of his food made her regret how long it was until her lunch break.

Things slowed down after that, so she drifted up and down the avenues with her light bar turned on. A lot of her nights were like this. It seemed like all of Manhattan decided to shift positions all at the same time and, once they got to the new place, they decided to stay there. Movement ebbed and flowed in unpredictable ways. But sooner or later, if she stuck with it, eventually an arm would go up and she'd be shuttling off to Chinatown or back to Chelsea.

Her lunch break came at ten o'clock. Five and a half hours of crawling the streets of the city, and she still had most of the night to go. She went back to Katz's and got a chicken salad sandwich. She drove to Delancey Street and parked next to the Williamsburg Bridge and sat on the hood of the cab to watch the traffic going across the river to Brooklyn.

She heard Mick's voice come over the radio. "Rafferty? Are you out there, I think this is when you usually your lunch break."

She reluctantly slid off the hood and got back behind the wheel. She sucked the mayo off her thumb before reaching for the mic.

"You do know what the words 'lunch break' mean, right, Mick?"

"Yeah, sorry, but I got a VIP call and I figured if I could send you instead of any of the other apes I have available, it would be better for everyone."

Rafferty wouldn't pretend she wasn't impressed by the idea of a VIP. "You're having me pick up a celebrity? Anyone I know?"

"Leonard Cohen."

"No kidding." She laughed. "I took someone to the Chelsea Hotel earlier tonight."

Mick gave a short, sharp laugh. "It's kismet, then. He's waiting for you at Radio City Music Hall, and he's heading to JFK."

Rafferty whistled. "Hell of a fare."

"Yeah, it's your lucky night. Are you a fan?"

"Yeah, I've got an album or two."

Mick said, "Well, don't embarrass me. Go on, he's waiting now."

Rafferty retrieved her trash from the hood of the cab and finished her drink. She was surprised that someone like Cohen wouldn't have a private driver, but she wasn't going to look a gift horse in the mouth. Radio City Music Hall to JFK Airport would be close to fifteen dollars. And if she kept her mouth shut and acted professionally, she felt like the singer would be a very generous tipper.

She pulled out of the lot humming a song about oral sex at the Chelsea Hotel, just to get it out of her system before she picked up her passenger.

After going to the airport and back, the cab was running on a quarter tank. She could conceivably keep going for another few trips, but she didn't like pushing it that far. Mick liked them to come back to the garage for that, and it was so much cheaper and easier than trying to find a station.

She had started humming again after Cohen got out of the cab. He'd been very quiet and still during the ride, to the point where she thought he might have fallen asleep. When they arrived, he handed her twenty dollars on top of the fare and said, "Thank you very much," before he disappeared. It wouldn't win any celebrity stories when she was hanging out with the other drivers, and it definitely wasn't the kind of thing her friends wanted to hear when they asked her if she'd ever had anyone famous in her cab. But it had been a highlight of her year, and it made her want to be a bigger fan of his music.

When she arrived at the garage, she beeped her horn and waited. After a minute, the new mechanic stepped out. She saw Rafferty waiting and waved her forward.

Rafferty rolled into the maintenance bay. It was where the cabs were washed, gassed up, and generally given their physicals before being sent back out onto the road.

"Need a top-up?"

Rafferty said, "That'd be great. Thanks."

Elise went to the pump and fitted the handle into the tank. Rafferty stayed behind the wheel and used the time to fill out her trip sheet. Pick-up time, pick-up location, length of trip, and then the same information for the drop-off. It was tedious, but Mick and the cashier both insisted on it. She knew it was important to keep track of all the minutiae just in case an issue cropped up, or if there was a bookkeeping problem, but it was honestly the worst part of the job. Who knew driving a car all night would involve paperwork?

"I hear you had a celebrity tonight."

Rafferty looked out the window, twisting to look back at where Elise was leaning against the back bumper.

"Yeah."

"I've never listened to him much. Is he any good?"

"Cohen? Yeah. He's great." She faced forward again.

Elise was quiet for almost a minute. "So does that happen often?"

"Driving Leonard Cohen to the airport?"

"Picking up celebrities?"

Rafferty shrugged. "Sure. It's Manhattan."

"Who's the most famous person you've ever driven somewhere?"

Rafferty's mind struggled to focus on the numbers. Miles, fares, street names. "Uh, I don't know. Cohen is pretty high up there."

"Ah. Okay." Elise was silent again for long enough for Rafferty to hope she was done. "I'd love to meet a celebrity like that. Not, like, bumping into them on the street or whatever. But a car ride. That's real time spent with a person. You can almost get to know a person during a car ride, you know?"

"Uh-huh," Rafferty muttered, still trying to focus on her paper instead of whatever Elise was talking about.

The pump clicked. "Oops, here you go." Elise returned the handle to the pump and twisted the gas cap back on. "All right. You're all set."

"Aces." Rafferty put away her paperwork. "Thanks."

"Sure. All part of the job. See you around."

"Yeah, probably."

Rafferty pulled forward and out of the maintenance bay. Once she was clear, she blew out air as if she'd been holding her breath the entire time she'd been inside. It was always a headache returning to home base just to get refueled, but it was going to be a nightmare if she had to deal with that chatterbox every time she was running low. Maybe it was just first day nerves and she would settle down once she'd gotten into the groove of the place. Or maybe Rafferty would have to try and work around the new girl's schedule so she could avoid her as much as possible. She still wanted to be friends with the woman. It would be so nice to have someone to back her up against the testosterone of the garage.

But lord, did she have to be such a pest?

CHAPTER TWO

NEW YORK may have been the city that never slept, but every night it went very quiet and calm around two-thirty. Still, it was easy to find people in need for someone who knew where to look. Lights were still on in a good number of office buildings, sidewalks were lit by windows of mostly empty twenty-four hour businesses. Rafferty had to wake up a third-shift nurse when they got to her building. An anchor for a local morning news show got into her backseat in a T-shirt and sweatpants, the suit he was going to wear on television draped across his lap in a garment bag.

When she finally reached the end of her shift, her route was blocked by a street sweeper. She carefully skirted around the blockade and drifted into the garage. The day shift cabbies, men she didn't know and never interacted with, were waiting. The end of her day meant the start of theirs. The interior of the cab would get a quick scrub-down, a mechanic would refill the gas tank, and Cab 582 would be back out on the streets in under half an hour.

She was surprised to see the new mechanic was still there, bent under the open hood of a cab. She handed in her keys and walked over.

"They're legally required to let you go home sometimes," she said. "You know that, right?"

Elise leaned out to see who was speaking to her and smiled.

"Oh hi!" She straightened up and reached for a rag. "I did go home for a little bit. And I'm going home after I finish up here. He said that they need mechanics on every shift, so I could have my choice. I figured I would see what each shift was like before I decided."

"So you've been here for twenty-four hours?"

"No!" Elise laughed and scanned the walls for a clock.

Rafferty wore a clunky man's watch and held out her left arm so Elise could see it.

"Oh! Oh, wow, that's huge. And lovely." She leaned in to read the time. "Oh, so yeah, actually I've only been here for about twenty hours. Yeah." She straightened up and shrugged. "I wasn't working the whole time, though. They made me go home at halftime. I think just so Mick wouldn't feel guilty."

"And you're sure you've been on the clock this whole time?"

"Oh yeah. We got that all locked in before I even touched an engine."

Rafferty was glad to hear that. The bosses at Achilles were trustworthy, for the most part, but they were also keen to save as much money as possible, whenever possible. She wouldn't put it past them to claim Elise had been working on a trial basis or as an apprentice.

"Did you make a decision?"

"I think so, yeah. I kind of like the night shift. It's quieter. A lot calmer. And..." She glanced toward the day shift, then stepped closer to Rafferty so she could lower her voice. "You all seem like the best group of drivers. The day crew doesn't even have a woman driver."

Rafferty chuckled. "Yeah. We're about as rare as female mechanics. It could be fun having you around. Maybe it'll even the odds against the macho bullshit."

"I'll do what I can. It's nice to meet you, Sally."

"Don't... it's Rafferty. Or Raff."

Elise swept her finger in the air like she was making a note. "Rafferty. Got it."

She tossed off a quick goodnight to Mick as she passed, then headed out to her own car. One last trip before she could call it a night. She considered going to a bar, maybe killing an hour or two until sunrise getting drunk and hustling a few pool games. But she could already feel exhaustion creeping in at the corners.

So even though she knew she wouldn't be able to fall asleep while it was still dark out, she aimed herself for home and prepared herself to stare at the TV like a zombie for a few hours.

She was alone, and everyone she would see that day would be a stranger.

Elise lay in bed and stared at the ceiling as she considered that fact. She was still getting used to the idea of sleeping during the daylight hours and working all night. She had blackout curtains in her bedroom, a suggestion from one of the drivers that she'd found extremely useful. She didn't like the way he'd given the advice, however. Almost as if he was trying to invite himself over to help install them. The idea of him being in her personal space finally made her uncomfortable enough to propel her out of bed.

She could hear her neighbors through the bathroom wall, and voices out in the hallway. People coming home from work, watching television, fighting. Her apartment was a shithole, especially compared to what she'd left behind. The entire apartment would have fit in the master bedroom of her old home. Hell, it basically *was* a master bedroom. Her bed was in what she would have called a closet, there was an ensuite bathroom, and the furniture had to be strategically placed to create the illusion of a dining room. The kitchen was just a counter along one wall that ended in a fridge.

But it was all hers. That fact alone was big enough to make up for any inconveniences or shortcomings.

Elise had been working at the Achilles Cab Company for a week. She could feel herself starting to adjust. She wasn't quite there yet. Her body still tried to wedge itself back into normal cycles. Exhaustion crept in around two in the morning. Her eyes sometimes refused to stay closed after noon. But she was confident that a few more days of breakfast at three in the afternoon would do the trick.

Today was her day off. Normally she would spend the time lounging around the house, reading or listening to music, but she needed to be active at the right hours or she'd undo all her adjustments. She needed to do laundry. Her building didn't have machines, but she'd found a laundromat within walking distance when she first chose the apartment. She loaded up her dirty clothes, chose a book to read while she waited, and headed out.

The laundromat was in a deep, narrow storefront. The round faces of the silver machines lining either wall made her feel like she was walking down the middle of a submarine, the portholes looking out on an oddly suds-filled ocean. There was only one other customer present when she arrived and, as she had quickly learned was the big-city custom, she ignored her presence as she went to the change machine and got some quarters.

It was only after she started her load and looked for a place to sit when she realized she knew the other customer. She'd only seen Rafferty a few times without a cap, and her hair being down disguised her enough that she had to move closer to make sure it was really her. She was reading a comic book, dressed in a white T-shirt that said I'M A PEPPER tucked into blue jeans.

She must have sensed Elise staring at her because she looked up. She looked irritated, then surprised, and then her face shifted to a neutral expression that Elise couldn't read.

Elise smiled and lifted her hand in a half-hearted wave. "Hey. Hi there."

"Hi." Rafferty looked around as if she was trying to find someone else to talk to. They were still alone. Even the attendant's booth was vacant. "So," she finally said. "I guess you live around here."

"Yeah, just around the corner. We must be neighbors."

"Guess so."

"Maybe some night we could carpool to the garage."

Rafferty nodded absently. "Sure. Maybe."

Elise tried to think of something else to say, or for Rafferty to continue the conversation, but the silence stretched on. She finally gave up waiting and took a seat that left a good buffer between them. She took out her book and flipped through to her bookmark.

"What are you reading?"

Elise tried not to look too excited about the question. She held the book up to show off the cover. "*Woman on the Edge of Time.* It's science-fiction. It's about a woman who can communicate with the future." She felt embarrassed saying it out loud. "It's kind of dorky."

Rafferty held up her comic. "I'm reading *Spider-Man.* Let's not call anything dorky."

Elise laughed. "I hear Spider-Man is pretty good, though. He, um, he just changed his costume to an all-black one, right?"

"Yeah," Rafferty said, lowering the book back to her lap. "I miss the red and blue, though."

"Don't mess with a classic."

"Right on," Rafferty said.

Elise decided that was a natural end to the conversation and didn't try to continue on. She focused on her book and let the hum of the machines drown out the street noise coming in through the window.

She'd only read half a chapter when Rafferty got up and transferred her clothes from a washer to a dryer. Elise kept her head down but looked up from the page to watch her. Something about the way she moved, the way her tight T-shirt was tucked into her jeans, triggered a long forgotten memory, but she forced herself to look away before she could grab onto it.

The cabbie was standoffish at work, quiet even when she was hanging out with the other drivers. There was a table in the garage where they could play games to pass the time. Rafferty would join in, she'd laugh at their jokes and tell stories, but there was always something performative about it. As far as Elise could tell, Rafferty was only doing the bare minimum of social interaction to avoid being labeled as a frosty bitch.

Maybe she was just a quiet person. Nothing wrong with that. Elise had actually very much enjoyed just sitting silently with her while they read their books. She wished there was a way she could convey that without sounding creepy. "If you ever want to read near someone and not talk…"

Rafferty came back after starting the dryer. She left the comic book on the seat next to her. Elise glanced over to see if she had anything else to help pass the time, but she kept her hands folded in her lap, staring at the posted rules and instructions hanging on the far wall.

Elise closed her book on her thumb and held it up. "Want to trade?"

"Pardon?"

"You finished your book. You could read a chapter of mine if you want, and I could see what Spider-Man is getting up to."

Rafferty looked like she wanted to refuse, but she looked at the book. "Science-fiction?"

"Time travel. Mental institutions."

"Sounds fun." She picked up her comic and held it out. "Thanks. I appreciate it."

Elise handed her book over and took the comic. "Don't worry about it. I'll be here longer than you anyway. Just don't lose my place."

Rafferty tapped the bookmark and nodded.

Elise opened the comic and scanned the first page. She had never actually read a comic book before and she'd half expected it to be like the Sunday newspaper pages. She was surprised to find it was an actual narrative, with an ongoing story that spanned the whole book. She mostly skimmed the dialogue and focused on the art, which really was pretty good.

The dryer buzzed. Rafferty put the book down and went to retrieve her clothes. When she crouched down to open the machine, Elise found her eyes drawn to the curve of Rafferty's thighs and the way she filled out the seat of her jeans.

Suddenly she realized what memory had been tugging at her mind when she ogled Rafferty earlier: Mrs. Pumpelly, her tenth grade English teacher. Tight sweaters. Khaki pants. Every time she turned her back to write on the board, Elise had been transfixed by the way her body moved. She wasn't curvy in the slightest, but something about the way she stretched and how her hips swayed when she erased the chalk...

Elise flinched hard when another buzzer sounded. She had a brief fear that some alarm had gone off, but she quickly realized it was actually just her clothes finishing the wash cycle. She cleared her throat and went to transfer everything to the dryer. She was grateful for the opportunity to get Rafferty out of her line of sight for a few minutes.

"That book is pretty good," Rafferty said, folding her clothes as she placed them into her basket.

"Uh yeah. Yeah, um, I'm liking it so far." She glanced over her shoulder. Rafferty was facing away from her, folding a T-shirt. "If you'd like, I can bring it in to work when I'm finished. Let you borrow it."

"Really? That would be great. Thanks."

"You're welcome." She fed quarters into her dryer and went back to the seat, then turned back to Rafferty. "Are there any good places to eat around here?"

Rafferty seemed surprised by the question. "You've lived here at least a week, right?"

"Yeah. But I've been doing the home-cooking thing. Well. Sandwiches and spaghettiOs. But I figure if I want to stick around I should venture out a bit farther. You probably know all the best places, right?"

"Sure." Rafferty leaned against the machine. "It depends on what you're in the mood for, really. If you want a burger and fries, go to Russell's. If you're looking for something a little nicer, there's a place called Red House a few blocks away."

"I'm kind of in the mood for Chinese."

"Evelyn's," Rafferty said without hesitation. "It's fantastic, no one else even compares. It's not far from here. Just down the street."

Elise nodded. "I'll keep that in mind. Thanks."

"No problem."

Elise went back to her seat and picked up her book. Rafferty finished folding her clothes and lifted the basket, resting it against her hip. She started for the door, but Elise stopped her.

"You forgot *Spider-Man*."

"Right," Rafferty said with a chuckle. She made her way over and took the comic, placing it on top of her laundry. She looked down at it, then looked at Elise. "I have a confession to make. I saw you come in, and I was kind of hoping you wouldn't recognize me. I don't like talking to people when I do my laundry. But I'm glad you showed up. This was nice."

Elise smiled. "I thought it was nice, too."

"I'm here most Saturdays around the same time. It's good, because there aren't a lot of people here this time of day. I wouldn't mind a little company if you showed up again next week."

"I'll keep that in mind."

Rafferty nodded. "All right. See you at the garage."

"See you there."

She watched Rafferty leave, then twisted to watch her through the front windows. Those tight jeans. That damn I'M A PEPPER shirt...

Once Rafferty was out of sight, Elise jumped from her seat and went to the vending machine she'd spotted at the back of the room. She fed her coin into the slot, bought a can of Dr. Pepper, and drank it like she'd just returned from the desert.

CHAPTER THREE

"SO WHAT do you think her story is?" Doc asked.

"Who?" Bob Groom looked at his cards and replaced two of them.

Doc scoffed. "What do you mean 'who'? I say 'her,' and one of the two women we both know is sitting at the table, so I'm obviously not talking about *her*."

Rafferty waved her cards like a Southern belle's fan. "Just honored to be part of the conversation, fellas."

"The new mechanic," Doc clarified, for anyone who wasn't following.

Sajan Harit, who went by the name "Hugh" for his "American friends who try so very hard," turned to look toward the row of cabs. Frank Burke and Tim Kuberski looked as well. Rafferty decided it wouldn't be weird if everyone else was looking, so she did as well. At the moment Elise was in the back of Cab 333 wiping down the seat before it was sent out again. The position unfortunately gave all the drivers at the table an unobscured view of her jumpsuit stretched across her rear end.

"What makes you think she has a story?" Tim asked. He already sounded bored with the topic. He listlessly shuffled his cards.

Doc said, "Well, look at her. She's gotta be pushing forty. And

Mick told me she said this is her first job as a mechanic. Someone starts a new job at that age, they got a story."

Frank looked at Rafferty. "She told you anything?"

"Why would she tell *me* anything?"

He shrugged. "Girls talk. They gossip. They peck-peck-peck-peck."

Rafferty gestured at the men circling the table. "And what exactly do you call this?"

"Research," Bob Groom said.

"It's gossip," Tim conceded, shifting his cigar to the other side of his mouth. "But you gotta admit, sweetheart, you girls made it into an art form."

She smiled despite herself. Tim was the oldest and wisest of the cabbies. He would bristle if anyone called him an enlightened man - or god forbid, a feminist - but he was the only one there willing to take a step back and see things from Rafferty's point of view. She respected him for the attempt, even if he didn't always nail the landing.

"She hasn't said anything to me." She wasn't keen on telling anyone about their run-in at the laundromat. "She probably just wanted a change of pace. Sick of being... I don't know. A waitress or a secretary or something."

"Women can be more than just waitresses and secretaries, Sal," Tim scolded sarcastically. "I'm surprised at you."

She flipped him off.

Mick's voice interrupted the round. "Rafferty, you're getting 333 tonight."

"My lucky number," she said, tossing her cards down.

She went to the cage to retrieve her keys and crossed the garage. Elise had finished cleaning out the backseat of the cab and stopped when their paths crossed.

"There wasn't anything horrible in the cab this time," Elise reported. "Just giving it a once-over. It's all good as new for you."

"I appreciate it. How's the book?"

"Pretty good! I'm almost finished. I'll bring it in tomorrow or the next night."

Behind Rafferty, at the card table, Doc said, "See? Gossiping! It's in their genes."

Elise looked at the men, confused, and looked at Rafferty for an explanation.

Rafferty rolled her eyes and waved them off. "Ignore them.

Men."

"Right. Well, have a good night."

Rafferty touched the brim of her cap and stepped around Elise. There was no particular reason the guys couldn't know she and Elise had run into each other outside the garage. She ran into them all the time. She and Tim shopped at the same grocery store. She'd see Frank at the movies once, acting like a doddering old grandpa to a little girl he'd never once mentioned to the other cabbies. Manhattan could be a very small town sometimes. Run-ins were to be expected.

But their behavior just now only confirmed she was doing the right thing by not talking about it. They would make jokes, crude comments, tease them. It was better to just deny them any ammunition.

She also wanted to keep the encounter secret because they would want details, and she wasn't entirely sure how she felt about the details. She'd gone to the library to see if they had a copy of the book Elise had been reading. When she asked the librarian about it, the older woman had snorted, eyed her suspiciously, and went back to stocking shelves.

"We don't stock *that kind* of literature."

"What kind?"

The woman had looked at her again, determined she was genuinely confused, and leaned in to whisper her response.

"*Queer* literature. Full of loose women and wild morals. Feminist claptrap."

Rafferty had oversold her surprise and thanked the woman for the information. "I won't be wasted my time with that, then."

Since then, the questions rolled through her mind at regular intervals. Did Elise know what the book contained? She must have. It would be in the summary, or she would have had to go to a specialist store to get it. It had been a copy she owned, right? She remembered the cover had been curled a bit, the spine broken. Maybe she'd gotten it at a stoop sale and had no idea what the subject matter was. It had looked like an ordinary science-fiction novel.

But what if she *did* know?

What if Elise Herald had deliberately chosen a book with queer characters?

No. If she'd known, she never would have been reading it so casually in public. And she wouldn't have offered it to someone she barely knew. She would have kept it to herself.

Unless it had been a test, to see how Rafferty reacted to it.

Rafferty sighed and snapped out of her own mind. Someone was flagging her down and she intended to spend the next few hours on autopilot, weaving across the island. If she focused, she could make it through the entire shift without having any thoughts more complicated than the quickest route to the Empire State Building.

Rafferty finished her shift in high spirits. Between the leasing fee to the cab company and paying for her own gas, it was possible to drive all night just to break even. This night was one of the good ones. She managed to reimburse herself early with a trip to Queens, booking a return far to the Battery, and spending the rest of the night with a nearly steady flow of passengers in and out of the backseat of her cab. She'd barely had time to stop for lunch so she ended up working straight through. On her way back to the garage, she picked up some empanadas to eat at the garage.

She was almost finished when Elise, already changed out of her coveralls, went to the cage and asked the cashier if he could change a five. The Reverend shook his head as he opened the register and traded her bill for coins.

"You gotta start carrying change, girl."

"I know, I know," she said. "I'm almost looking forward to the subway raising the fare so it will be a full dollar."

"You know they'd just make it a buck-ten," the Reverend said. "Just to screw with people."

She laughed and shook her head. "Thanks, Reverend." She turned away, saw Rafferty at the table, and nodded hello to her. "Good night, Rafferty."

"Hold on," Rafferty said. "You need fare for the subway?"

"Yeah. Exact change. It's such a hassle..."

Rafferty cut her off with a wave of her hand. "You take the subway home? At four in the morning? How have you not been murdered?"

Elise stammered. "I-I don't... I don't know. Just lucky, I guess."

"Hang out for a second and I'll drive you home."

"Oh! You don't have to do that."

Rafferty said, "If tonight is the night someone with a knife is waiting to mug you, I'll feel terrible for not doing it." She pushed out the chair across from her. "Sit. I'm almost done here."

Elise hesitated, then sat down. "I appreciate it. The station really isn't that far."

"I honestly don't know how you've escaped unscathed so far." Rafferty shook her head. "It's almost miraculous."

Elise had paled slightly since she sat down. "Gosh. I just thought the horror stories in the media were exaggerations or, or just people blowing things out of proportion. I had no idea."

"You know this neighborhood is called Hell's Kitchen, right?"

"Yes. But that's just a name."

Rafferty shrugged. She looked past Elise at the cashier. "Hey, Rev. Did you put in a good word with the Big Man upstairs? Keep her safe?"

The Reverend shook his head. "Never been to church, don't care what y'all call me."

"Hm." Rafferty tossed her food wrapper into the brown paper bag, then stood up. "Okay. Let's get outta here."

They walked outside to the parking lot.

"Our shifts don't always end at the exact same time," Rafferty said, "but if you don't mind hanging around, we could make this a regular thing."

"I'd hate to be an imposition."

"You're practically a neighbor, right? I'm more annoyed thinking about all those nights you spent alone on the subway. Jesus."

"It wasn't that bad." She got into the passenger seat of Rafferty's car. "Okay, there *have* been a couple of times when people got on and I felt a little..."

Rafferty waited.

"Tense. But mostly it was just homeless people getting out of the weather. I just left them alone and they left me alone."

"You got lucky. Damn lucky."

She pulled out of the lot and headed north.

"Have you ever been robbed?"

"On the subway or in the cab?"

"Either."

"Hell yes," Rafferty said. "I've had guns pulled on me, knives, fingers in coat pockets. One guy tried to threaten me with a coat hanger. I'm not sure what the logic was on that one."

Elise said, "Wow. I would be so terrified."

Rafferty shrugged. "You get used to it."

"You get used to people pulling guns on you, demanding your

money." She laughed and shook her head. "No way."

"It's just like everything else. Once it's happened enough times, you stop being startled by it."

Elise was still shaking her head. "Well, *I* still think you must be very brave."

Rafferty smiled, proud despite herself. "Thanks."

The silence dragged out between them for two blocks. They sat at a red light, the street clear in all directions but Rafferty couldn't ignore it.

"So. Where are you from?"

Elise started to say something, stopped, then said, "Upstate. And not to be rude, can we just leave it at that for now?"

"Sure," Rafferty said.

"You?"

"Chicago. Moved here about ten years ago, right after high school."

Elise said, "How'd you end up driving up a cab?"

Rafferty bristled. "I didn't 'end up' doing anything. It's a job. It's a good job. Maybe not the most glamorous or best paying, but necessary. It's a great way to learn about the city. I've seen more of New York than people who've lived here their entire lives. I *like* driving my cab. And it really bugs me when people think it's a fallback position or some kind of failing to do what we do."

"I'm sorry." Elise's voice was meek. "I didn't mean it like that."

Rafferty sighed and rubbed her hand over her face. "No. I'm sorry. I lashed out, because a lot of people *do* mean it like that. The guys get the question a lot, too, but I think being a woman makes it a hundred times worse. This isn't a job women typically do. So everyone feels the need to point that out to me when they get in the backseat. Well, not everyone."

"Men," Elise said at the same time Rafferty said it.

"Exactly," Rafferty said. "Even if you had meant it that way, it's not entirely crazy to assume. My mother called New York 'Zero City.' She said everyone comes here with a dream. They want to hit Broadway, get discovered. But the city gives you nothing, and eventually you become nothing. For every person who makes it, there are a hundred thousand who fail. Pretty soon you just turn into a nobody waiting for a big break that will never come. Zeroes."

Elise was watching the street roll by outside the window. "That's depressing."

"I guess you could look at it that way. But I didn't come here for anything other than to be here. To live in Manhattan. I earn a living at a job I really enjoy. I make enough to feed myself and take an occasional vacation. A very occasional vacation. I consider myself a success. And on top of that, I've easily given rides to hundreds, maybe thousands of people. And do you know how many of them I'd call zeroes?"

"None?"

Rafferty smiled. "Well. No, there have been a couple of duds... Let's say ten percent."

Elise laughed. "I get your point. You're lucky, then."

"What about you?" Rafferty asked, wanting to change the subject before they focused too much on her luck, or lack thereof. "Did you come here chasing some big dream?"

"Oh. No, I'm not particularly talented at anything. I'm really good at fixing cars, because as soon as I learned to drive, I was terrified of breaking down somewhere and being stranded. I didn't want to rely on some man to come save me. So I learned as much as I could about engines. I guess most of it just wound up sticking. I needed a job when I got here, and Achilles posted an ad asking for mechanics. It made sense. If there's one thing Manhattan has an endless supply of, it's cars."

"True. I'm glad it worked out. It's actually pretty nice having another woman around the garage for a change."

"Same. I was worried about spending all night, every night, with a bunch of men. Even if you're out on the road for the entire shift, it's nice to know you'll be around." She pointed. "Oh, I'm the next right up here."

Rafferty pulled into the turn lane. "If I ask you for money when we get there, ignore me. It's just habit."

Elise laughed. "So I shouldn't tip you?"

"Oh, no, tips are always appreciated."

"It's right here on the left," Elise said, still chuckling.

Rafferty pulled to the curb. "Wait, you live here? You know there's a..." She cut herself off before she could finish the thought.

"What?" Elise asked.

"No, uh. I was just... I was going to say there's a really great, um, Chinese place nearby. But they closed down a while back."

"Oh. That's a shame."

Rafferty nodded. "That's one of the downsides of this city. As soon as you get used to it being one shape, suddenly it's something completely different. I don't know how non-cabbies manage to keep up with it all."

"Thanks for the ride. And the conversation. You really don't have to do this every night."

"I wouldn't be able to sleep thinking about you on the subway. Maybe on the weekends when our shift ends at eight AM. That should be safe. But the middle of the night?" She shook her head. "I'm happy to do it. Especially since we're so close."

"Oh, we *are* close? I wasn't sure how central the laundromat was."

Rafferty nodded and gestured vaguely ahead. "I live just down the way here. Not far at all."

"That's a relief. As long as it isn't an imposition."

"Not at all. I'll see you at the garage."

Elise nodded. "And I'll probably finish the book tonight before bed, so I'll bring that along."

"Can't wait. Goodnight."

"Night."

Elise got out of the car. Rafferty waited until she was safely in the lobby of the building before she pulled away from the curb.

As soon as she was alone again, she immediately began to cross-examine herself and her motives. Yes, the subway was dangerous at night. But the Guardian Angels were doing a good job to keep crime low, despite what the mayor said. Elise had managed this long without incident so maybe Rafferty was just overreacting and creating an unnecessary fear in her.

If that was the case, she'd have to admit that the main reason she'd offered Elise the ride was because she wanted to spend time with her. And admitting that meant that she was starting to like the mechanic. Maybe more than she should. She tried to think about if she would've made the same offer to Tim, or Hugh, or Bob Groom. No, because they wouldn't have accepted the offer anyway, because "women don't protect men like that." They would have taken the subway out of spite if she'd said anything.

She sighed deeply. There was no point analyzing herself or dissecting her reasons behind stepping up. The fact was she'd been present, she'd seen someone in need, and she had been in a position to reduce the chance Elise became a victim. That was all. Plain and simple.

What was less plain and simple was the thing she stopped herself from saying when she discovered Elise's address. She had almost pointed out there was a laundromat just around the corner, about half the distance from the one they were supposed to meet again in a few days. It was a bigger, nicer place, and it would cut Elise's walk in half. A real friend would have told her about it even if it meant they wouldn't get a chance to hang out again. A real friend wouldn't have hesitated to put Elise's needs before her own.

Rafferty didn't want to think about what that made her.

Elise waited in the lobby of her building until she was absolutely sure Rafferty was out of sight. Even then, she peeked through the window next to the door before she actually went outside. She appreciated the ride, but it had come on the worst possible day. There was something she had planned to do at the subway station and she'd been dreading it. Part of her wanted to take Rafferty's offer as a sign from the universe, but she also knew that was her cowardly side. She couldn't let that side win, even if that meant venturing back out into the night.

There was a payphone at the corner. A streetlight was close enough for her to see the keypad, and she dialed the number from memory. She put the ice-cold receiver to her ear and closed her eyes.

"Don't pick up," she whispered on every rattling buzz of the connection being made. "Don't pick up. Don't pick up."

A click, a rustle, the clearing of a throat. "Hello?"

Michael's voice. Elise wasn't prepared for how much it would twist her inside to hear him. She opened her mouth to say something, but words failed her. She hadn't practiced this part.

"Hello?" he said again. "Who is this?"

Elise turned her back on the phone booth and looked up at the building behind her. A few windows were lit; there was always someone awake in this city.

"Elise...?"

She jumped and looked at the phone. Had she made a noise? Said something without realizing it? How could he have possibly known?

He was still talking. "~whatever happened, wherever you are, just come home. We can talk about this. We can figure something out together. You can't just vanish like~"

She hung up. She stared at the phone, half-expecting it to start ringing. When it remained silent, she turned and walked away from the booth. She'd planned a whole speech. Something so he wouldn't worry, something that would officially cut ties between her and where she'd come from. But when the moment came, she could feel herself buckling. Giving in. All she could think about was how much easier it would be to just go home and polish over the cracks. Settle in again.

Maybe hanging up the phone let her cowardly side win. But also, maybe it was the only way she could find the strength to stay in the city.

CHAPTER FOUR

"SO THIS guy I know told me about this crazy chick he had in his cab..."

"Oh, here we go," Rafferty muttered. "A 'guy I know' story."

There was no card game tonight, so she was working on a crossword puzzle. Doc Beeler was sitting to her right, and Frank Burke was at her left. Bob Groom had immediately launched into his latest story as he dropped into the seat across from her.

"No, hand to God, all right? Guy's dispatcher backed him up and everything. So, okay, he picks this couple up from the Yacht Club, okay? Rich prick and trophy wife. Lady looks like a damn supermodel~"

"How do you know what she looked like, Bobby?"

"Don't interrupt, Raff, okay? My friend told me the whole story." He laughed and shook his head. "And believe you me, once you hear the story, you'll know why he remembered every detail. So, okay, he picks them up. They're both dressed to the nines. He can't stop sneaking peeks at her in the rearview. The guy is just going off on her, all right? How she was rude to his friends and judging them all or whatever. She's just taking it all. It ain't her first rodeo, right? Made her choice when she married the prick."

"Sure," Frank said.

"So he's only going a few blocks, but he asks my friend~"

"He got a name?" Doc asked.

Bob stumbled over the story. "Wha, who? The rich prick?"

"This friend of yours," Doc said.

"It doesn't matter. Anyway, he's only going a few blocks, but he asks my friend, *Larry*, to take his wife all the way home to their townhouse in Gramercy Park after dropping him off. So they've got a little over a mile to go. All by themselves. So they get to talking. She's sorry for the language her husband used, Larry is sorry she has to deal with that, blah blah blah. They get to the townhouse, and all of a sudden, the lady realizes her husband had all the cash."

Doc faked a gasp. "Oh dear, what a pickle."

Rafferty chuckled softly.

"She tells Larry he can come inside while she gets some money~"

Mick interrupted the story by speaking over the intercom. "Rafferty, you've got 333 again."

"Thank God." She folded the newspaper and stuck it in her back pocket as she stood. She got the keys and passed by the table on her way to the cab. "Last time he picked them up at the Plaza and took her to the Dakota."

Bob looked confused. "Wait. Last time...?"

Doc said, "I think the time before that, it was LaGuardia and somewhere on the Upper West Side."

"Oh, who can remember," Frank said.

"Certainly not Bob," Rafferty said as she got into her cab.

She spotted Elise on her way out of the garage. Elise stepped out of her way and offered a shy wave, then a salute. Rafferty smiled and returned the wave as she passed by.

It had been a few days since they started carpooling home. The first few trips, they tried to force conversation. But Rafferty didn't really like talking about herself, and Elise didn't seem to *want* to talk about herself. Rafferty was fine with that. She didn't see any reason people had to be an open book, especially with their coworkers. She eventually told Elise that they didn't have to talk if she wanted to take advantage of the ride and get in a little nap.

So the past few nights, Elise had gotten into the passenger seat, folded her arm against the window to use it as a pillow, and slept for the few minutes it took to get from the garage to her apartment. Rafferty was surprised by how much she liked it. There was something calming about having a sleeping woman in the seat next to her. She also liked the moment of waking Elise up when they got to her apartment. A gentle shake on the shoulder, softly saying, "Hey, we're here." Seeing Elise's eyelids flutter and the moment of confusion before she sat up and stretched.

It was intimate. It was tender. It was... something she didn't want to focus much on, or get too accustomed to.

Her fares that afternoon into evening were the typical crowd. Workers heading home after a shift, college students, tourists. As the sun set, she started picking up couples preparing for a night out. She tried not to be jealous of their fancy outfits, the chic restaurants they directed her to. She didn't want that kind of evening. Slathering herself with makeup and then spending a week's pay on a mediocre meal didn't sound like a great night out to her.

It was close to midnight when a girl in a neon pink prom dress and tiara stepped off the curb to wave her down. The sash across her chest read BECCA in purple letters outlined with pink. Four other women dressed identically, sans tiara and with different names on their sashes, waited at the curb. Rafferty briefly considered the wisdom of picking them up and decided to risk it. She pulled over and Becca gathered her dress to hurry over.

She opened the back door and leaned in. "There's five of us. Is it okay if one rides up front?"

Rafferty hated that. But she appreciated that they had bothered to ask. Most passengers didn't, and some of them even tried to get in front when they were riding alone. *Don't make me ride all lonely back there. It's easier to talk this way anyway.*

"Sure," she said. "Thanks for checking."

"Holy shit." Becca straightened and turned back to the quartet. "Hurry! It's a *girl*! Come on!"

The prom dresses descended on Rafferty's cab, filling the back seat like a swarm of neon butterflies. Becca got in the front seat and twisted to face Rafferty.

"Okay! Hi! So. Obviously this is my bachelorette party. First, we're going to Lombardi's Pizza. Do you know where that is?"

"Nolita, right?" Rafferty said.

"Right!"

Rafferty pulled away from the curb. "Let's get going."

Becca said, "Okay, second!" She clapped her hands together. "So. We're going to a couple of places tonight. And it's, like, fate or something that we snagged a *girl cabbie*. I mean, tonight of all nights, we didn't need the male energy getting in the way, right? So, like, what would it cost to, to like buy you?"

"Becca!" one of the girls in the backseat shrieked.

"No, not like that! God, Meghan!" She rolled her eyes. "I mean, to have you, like, wait for us and leave the light to off-duty so no one will steal you away while we're celebrating."

Rafferty winced. She wanted to help, but she also couldn't waste an entire night just sitting in a parking lot while some sorority girls got wasted.

"How many places are you going?"

Becca pointed to someone in the backseat. "Judy, tell her!"

"After pizza, we're going to a little elite boutique on Greene Street that's open all night. From there we're going to a dance club called Shatter. Then the Empire State Building, and after that back to our hotel in Midtown."

Rafferty pictured the map in her mind. It covered a decent stretch of the island. She tried to calculate how much potential income she would lose if they spent thirty minutes to an hour at each place. There could be a lot of short trips, or one-way drives to Queens or Brooklyn with an empty cab on the ride back. She'd already had a decent night up to that point. So even if they were her last fare of the night, it wouldn't be that difficult to make it worth her while.

"You pay what's on the meter, plus ten bucks for every hour from now until I drop you off."

"Yes!" Becca said immediately, then looked into the backseat. "Linda, you're the banker tonight. Make sure we have enough to pay her, all right? Plus a big tip, because I know this is probably a pain in the ass for you."

Rafferty shrugged. "As long as none of you puke in my cab, we'll get along fine."

Becca laughed and pointed to one of the girls. "You heard her, Judy!"

"Oh shut up!"

"Okay, you got a deal, cabbie."

One of the girls in the backseat said, "Her name is Sally!" She tapped the license displayed on the partition. "Thanks for the ride, Sally!"

"We love you, Sally!" the other girls chimed in.

Rafferty choked down her instinctual reaction to correct them. Tonight, just for these girls, she could be Sally.

The bachelorette and her friends had turned into a very

lucrative night for Rafferty. First, when the girls finally emerged from Lombardi's, Becca handed Rafferty a slice of cheese pizza. "Not part of your tip, just to show our appreciation!" The other girls whooed their agreement.

Rafferty accepted gratefully and revealed she had spent her time well while they were inside. There was a map in her glove compartment, and she'd used it to chart a course of their itinerary.

"We can go the straightforward route, which is the cheap option and what I'd normally do. But if you want the scenic route, there are some detours I can take. It might be a bit more expensive~"

"Scenic route!" Becca insisted. "We're only here for three more days, and then who knows if we'll ever make it back!" She grabbed Rafferty's shoulder and squeezed. "Show us the city, Sally!"

So she set out. She took them around Washington Square Park so they could see the Arch on the way to the dance club. From there, another detour to show them the Flatiron Building, and let them get out to take pictures at the Madison Square Fountain. After that, they hit the Empire State Building, Times Square, and Rockefeller Center, all of which resulted in the girls climbing out of the cab to take photos. One of the girls, Meghan, seemed to have an inexhaustible supply of film. By Rafferty's estimate they took close to five hundred pictures by the time she headed for their hotel.

"You're the best, Sally," Becca said, slurring her words slightly from alcohol and exhaustion. The adrenaline of the night was starting to wear off. "Best driver ever."

"Best ever!" came a chorus from the backseat.

The meter ended up reading nine dollars, and the entire trip took three hours. Linda counted off forty dollars and Becca insisted on adding fifteen more as the tip. "I'm too drunk to do percentages, is that a good tip?" Rafferty assured her that it was. Becca kissed her hard on the cheek and thanked her again as she got out of the cab and followed her bridesmaids into the hotel.

Rafferty decided it was close enough to the end of her shift to call it a night, especially with the windfall from Becca and her girls. She drove back to the garage and turned in the cab, then settled in at the card table to start filling out the trip sheet. She'd taken notes on mileage and start-stop points in a notepad while she was waiting for the girls at each stop, but she needed something a little more polished for the official log.

She was almost finished when Elise slid into the chair across from her. "Hi."

"Hey there," Rafferty said.

"Bad shift?"

Rafferty looked up. "No... Why?"

Elise sat up straighter, clearly surprised. "Oh. No reason. You just looked bummed."

"I'm..." Rafferty ignored the urge to just claim she was fine and move on. Being honest with herself, she *was* a little upset. She tapped her finger on the trip sheet. "I had a bachelorette party in the cab tonight."

"Oof." Elise winced. "Someone get drunk? No one threw up, did they?"

"No! No, they were great. Really great. Included me in the whole thing, gave an amazing tip. They even bought me a slice of pizza."

Elise raised her eyebrows. "Wow! That sounds like a great night." She tilted her head to the side. "So why do you look like you just drove lead car in a funeral procession?"

Rafferty leaned back in her chair and sighed. "Because it was a great night. It was *their* great night. And before them, people going out for *their* fancy dates. Even the two hundred tourists going to the damn Statue of Liberty were seeing it for the first time. Making memories they'll cherish forever. And I was just driving everybody. I love my job, I really do. But some nights it's hard to forget that all I'm doing is making other people's great nights happen. I haven't had a great night of my own in a long time."

Elise reached across the table and rested her hand on top of Rafferty's. "I'm sorry. I never thought about how that must feel."

Rafferty shrugged. "It's no big deal. Just kind of a letdown."

"Sure. Sure."

Rafferty looked down at Elise's hand, still on hers. "Why aren't your hands ever disgusting?" She turned her hand over and lifted Elise's fingers. "You've been working on engines all night. These should be black as coal but they're so soft."

"Lava soap," Elise said. "It's magical. Scours away grease, dirt, everything, without chewing up your skin."

"Wow. That's amazing. Future soap."

"I think it's been around for about a hundred years."

"Huh. You learn something new every day." She let go of Elise's hand, cleared her throat. "I guess since you washed your hands, you're finished with your shift? I'll still drive you home, I just need to finish this up."

Elise nodded. "Okay. I don't mind waiting. As long as you don't mind..."

"We've been over this," Rafferty said. "I appreciate the company. And you can warn me if I start to get... what word did you use?"

"Bummed."

Rafferty smiled. "Yeah. Bummed."

Elise smiled back. "Deal."

Chapter Five

"DO YOU think it's true?"

Rafferty had thought Elise was asleep, as she usually was during the drive home. She was curled against the door, arm against the window as a pillow. She hadn't even lifted her head to ask her question.

"What?"

"That story Bob Groom was telling about the sexy lady from the Yacht Club."

"Oh that." Rafferty laughed. "The Yacht Club, or the Plaza, or the Governor's Mansion. Or on an all-night trip to the Hamptons..." She sighed and shook her head. "I think something like that *could* have possibly happened to a driver, at some point. This city, nothing is impossible. But it definitely didn't happen recently, and it didn't happen to Bob Groom's friend."

Elise made a quiet noise. She sat up and pushed her bangs out of her face. They simply fell back immediately.

"How about you?" Elise asked.

"What about me?"

"Has it ever happened..." She trailed off and looked out the window. After half a block, she faced forward again. "You know. With a passenger, have you ever...?"

Rafferty chuckled uncomfortably. "Uh."

"You don't have to answer that. I'm sorry. It's so inappropriate."

"No, it's fine." Rafferty shifted. "Yeah, it's happened."

Elise looked at her. "Really?"

"Yeah. It wasn't some letter to *Playboy* like whatever urban legend Bob Groom was telling." She decided to pretend it was only the one time, playing it safe. "It was New Years Eve. We were both lonely. It happened to be midnight, so we kissed. And when we got to the destination, I... I went inside. And I stayed there until the end of the shift."

"Wow."

Rafferty risked a look, trying to read her face. "Is that judgement in your voice, or...?"

"No. No, I don't know what it is. I've never done anything like that. I don't think poorly about you for doing it, but I also can't imagine what it would be like to do it."

"You're not..." It was her turn to struggle with words. "I mean, it's fine if you are. But, I mean, you've... had sex before, right?"

Elise laughed. "What? Yes. My god, I'm..." She nodded. "I'm not a virgin, Rafferty, god. I just meant casually. Outside of a relationship, outside of a commitment. With a *stranger*. I don't know if I could do it with someone I didn't know I could trust."

"That's not something to be ashamed of," Rafferty said. "It's admirable. Hell, the world might be a little better if more people had that attitude."

She pulled up in front of Elise's building. "Here we are."

"Yeah. Oh, have you started the book yet?"

"I haven't had a chance," Rafferty said. "I'm off tomorrow, so I'll probably get started on it when I get home."

"I can't wait to talk about it with you. Okay." She patted her thighs with both hands, then opened the door. She got out onto the curb, then leaned down into the open doorway. "If you're looking for something to do on your day off, we should get together and do something."

"Like what?"

Elise shrugged. "Get dinner. See a movie. I don't know. We'll think of something. It won't be hard to top laundry. You deserve a great night of your own."

Rafferty smiled, mostly to hide the fact her eyes were threatening to tear up. "That would be nice, Elise. I'll see what I can come up with. I usually sleep most of the day and wake up around three. I'll call you around, uh, five? See what we can figure out."

"Oh. I don't have a phone. I'll just be ready at five and we can figure it out on the road?"

"Works for me. See you tomorrow."

"See you then."

Elise closed the door and went into her building.

When Rafferty got home, she heated up a frozen dinner and started Elise's book at the built-in kitchenette while she ate. It was a very strange book, with a focus on mental illness and time travel, but she quickly decided she liked the weirdness. It was also very queer, with the future person being in a polyamorous relationship. The future, according to the book, was very open in terms of sexuality and personal freedom.

Rafferty had to wonder about the kind of person who would read a book like this. And on top of that, she had to wonder about a person who would loan it out knowing its message. If she passed it on to Doc Beeler, he would spread the rumor she was a lesbian before the end of the next shift. *You wouldn't believe the book she's reading. It's all about how the future is a utopia where the gays are in charge.*

Maybe Elise didn't realize the assumptions people would make about the book.

Or maybe she realized, but didn't care since it was Rafferty.

She got about two-thirds of the way through the book before her eyes demanded she stop and sleep. She left the book on the dinner table and went to bed, where she drifted off to thoughts about time travelers and a future where it didn't matter who she dreamed about sleeping next to her.

One thing Elise truly loved about her apartment was the bath. The landlord had been apologetic about the lack of shower, but she'd considered it a selling point. She loved taking baths. They were where she did her best thinking. That particular night she was thinking of what she could possibly suggest for her girls night out with Rafferty. She didn't know anywhere fun in the city. Hell, she didn't know anywhere at all except for the boring tourist magnets. Rafferty probably went to those places ten times per night, dropping off tourists and then picking them up again. There was no way she'd find that fun.

She sank both arms into the water, then lifted them up to

watch the cascade flow over her skin. Her knees stuck up like islands in front of her, and she rested her hands on them. She sank lower in the tub so that only her hands, knees, and face were exposed to air.

She was glad she could just lay here. She was glad she didn't have a telephone in the apartment, tempting her every minute with the possibility of being weak and calling Michael. She had a feeling that if she did call him, and if she did somehow summon up the courage to speak, Rafferty would be the only subject she'd be able to focus on.

Elise turned her hands over and brushed the backs against her thighs. *They're so soft.* Rafferty had said it while touching them, stroking the palm with her fingertips. Rafferty's hands were soft, too. But strong. Hour after hour of gripping the steering wheel, probably, guiding a ton of Detroit steel through the streets of New York. Strong hands... strong fingers...

The thought sent Elise's mind down paths that made her shudder. She bit her lip and pushed her knees together, dipping low enough to get all her hair wet before she sat up. She brushed the water out of her face and stared at the brown-orange tile across from her. She saw her reflection in the metal of the faucet. She was distorted and twisted in it, and somehow that made the decision easy.

It didn't matter what they did together. Rafferty already liked her, had already agreed to spend the time with her, and the details were secondary to spending time with each other outside of work.

She smiled as she felt the relief wash over her. She could relax and let her mind stop twisting around the problem, because it wasn't a problem. It was just a choice to be made, and there was no wrong answer. She was off the hook. They'd figure something out, even if they had to make decisions on the fly. Whatever happened, it was certain to be a great night.

When Rafferty arrived the next day, she had decided the best plan was no plan. She explained it to Elise as she pulled away from the curb. "We just drive. This is Manhattan, right? Eventually we're going to see somewhere we want to stop or something we want to see. So if we don't have a plan, we can just stop and spend as much time as we want."

"I think that sounds like an excellent idea. But are you sure you don't mind driving?"

"It's tricky, but I think I've got the hang of it."

Elise laughed. "No, but that's what I mean. You drive all day. I'd hate to make you just drive around on your day off."

Rafferty shook her head. "I find it relaxing. Especially with a passenger like you."

"Is that why you let me ride up front?"

"VIP status, for sure."

Elise said, "I'm honored."

"You should be. So..." She scanned the street. "Have you had a chance to do much sightseeing since you got to Manhattan? We can hit the main sights. The bachelorette party reminded me of how pretty this city can be."

"I took myself on a tour when I first got here. Central Park, Empire State Building, Statue of Liberty. It seems like such a tiny place on the map but then you get here... how'd they get everything on this little bitty island?"

"Magic," Rafferty said.

"I'd believe it." She leaned closer to the window and looked up to see the tops of the buildings. "You know, I've been thinking about that thing your mother said. Saying this is 'Zero City.' I think that's a good name, but not in the bad way like she meant it. No matter where you come here from, or what you're hoping for, everyone who comes here is starting at zero. Fresh start, clean slate, sweep the board and start over. It doesn't matter who you were before or where you came from. Zero. It's comforting."

Rafferty considered it. "That *is* comforting, when you put it that way."

Elise shifted in the seat. "I know you and the guys talk about me at the garage. Trying to figure out what my deal is. A woman on the edge of forty doesn't just appear out of thin air starting a new job in a new town without a backstory."

"The guys do that with everyone," Rafferty said. "And I'm curious, sure. But you clearly don't want to talk about it. I'm not going to make full disclosure a requirement for being a friend. You'll tell me when you're ready. Or not. I'm happy to start at zero with you."

"I appreciate that."

Rafferty said, "If you ever want to know their backstories, though, I'm more than happy to spill the beans. Frank has two ex-wives and four kids. He has another job stocking shelves at D'Agostino's. He says that's the job he uses to support himself, and driving the cab is to support the kids and pay his alimony. Doc Beeler was driving all over New York trying to find a job and one day he decided if he was going to spend all his time behind the wheel anyway, he might as well get paid for it."

"That's great," Elise chuckled. "Oh hey. That place looks nice. And there doesn't seem to be a crowd."

She was pointing at a bar with a simple neon sign reading BAR - POOL - DARTS. Rafferty looked at Elise to see if she was joking.

"Sometimes there's not a crowd for a reason."

"I know," Elise said. "But as long as this isn't a horrible neighborhood..."

Rafferty acknowledged it was decent enough. She didn't feel anxious about leaving her car unattended, for a little while, at least. And sometimes dives were a much better time than anything they'd find in a more reputable part of town. She pulled into a side lot and parked.

The sun was still up, but inside the bar was dark as midnight. Only a few lights were shining at the bar, with individual fixtures at each booth. The back part of the room was the most well-lit, because that was where the pool table, the dart board, and the unadvertised arcade games lived. A jukebox in the corner was playing "Rock 'n' Roll Fantasy" by Bad Company, but it wasn't so loud that they wouldn't be able to talk. The room was mostly empty save for a few barflies hunched over their drinks, so Rafferty sent Elise back to claim a game while she went to the bar for their drinks.

The bartender was a tall man with thinning curly hair. All of his features were tiny save for his ears, which seemed to have gotten the bulk of the genetics. He pushed two bottles of beer to her.

"Need quarters for the machines?" he asked, his words twisted by Brooklyn.

"Not yet. We'll see how the night goes."

"Sounds are all turned off on Pac-Man. Don't turn 'em on or we'll kick your butts out."

Rafferty nodded. "Understood."

She took the drinks back. Elise had taken down two pool cues and was examining the chalk square. Rafferty set the drinks down on a table and picked up her cue.

"You know how to play pool?"

"The community center had one where I grew up. They put it in a room without thinking about whether there would be room for people to actually make shots."

Elise laughed. "Seems like a fatal flaw."

"People tried their best, but I don't think we really got the full experience of the game. I think I get the gist of it. Enough for a friendly game, at least."

"We could play for drinks," Rafferty said. "If I win, you reimburse me for the drinks. If you win, it's my treat."

Elise smiled and nodded. "That seems fair enough."

Rafferty almost laughed. But she decided there were some rules about New York Elise would have to learn the hard way. Number one being, no one played 'friendly games' of pool in bars, and if anyone suggested betting, run far and fast. She almost felt bad about the ruse, even if it was for Elise's benefit.

Three games later, and in debt to Elise for two rounds, her goodwill had run out. "I'm going to start playing for real now," she declared as she circled the table.

"Oh thank God," Elise said. "I felt so bad when I thought you were actually trying to win."

Rafferty couldn't help but laugh. "Oh, you're evil! This whole time you've been evil." She bent to line up her next shot. "I bet your community center didn't even have a pool table."

"Oh, they did. But it was in a *huge* rec room. Who wouldn't check to make sure there's enough clearance for the cues?"

"What else did you lie about? Have you been in here before? Do you own this place? Is Big Ears your employee?"

Elise laughed. "No, I've never been here before. But I did hustle you, so I apologize for that. I won't hold you to the bet."

Rafferty shook her head. "No, we'll go one more. Double or nothing." She put her cue down on the table. "But not in pool. Darts."

"Oh. I've actually never played darts before." She pointed at the board. "How many points do I get for hitting the black part around the edge?"

"Oh, god, what have I done..." Rafferty went to retrieve the darts. "Just play, grease monkey. Around the clock, 1 to 25. Can you handle that?"

"I think I can figure it out."

Elise smiled, and it was different than most of her other smiles. This one involved tucking her bottom lip behind her top teeth, and Rafferty found it almost unbearably cute. She looked away before Elise caught her. She took aim with her first dart and launched it, hitting the 1 segment.

"Can I ask you something?"

"Is it about taking your scam to Atlantic City?" Rafferty threw her second and third darts. "Because I'm in, but we need to negotiate cuts. I'm fine with sixty-forty."

Elise laughed and shook her head. She stepped forward to take her turn. "No, it's about work. Mick, actually. I'm just curious why he wears those sunglasses all the time."

Rafferty's mood dampened slightly. "Oh. That's not really a 'fun' story. And I'm not sure it's my story to tell."

"Oh. If it's none of my business..."

"Well. I understand being curious. And it would be awkward to ask him." She considered her options and shrugged. "Okay. You know the chain-link fence around the parking lot? Where the cabbies leave their cars when we're on the shift?"

Elise nodded, somber now. She had only thrown one dart, but she seemed to have forgotten about the game. Rafferty nodded at the board, and Elise took the hint and made her next shot.

"That fence wasn't always there. One night, back when Mick was still driving, some guy was waiting out there to mug him when he got back at the end of a shift." She shook her head. "Anyway, the guy went after Mick with a crowbar."

"Oh my god."

"He was hurt pretty bad," Rafferty said. "Most of it was stuff that could heal, but he lost his left eye. He didn't want a glass eye, and he thought eyepatches made him look like a cartoon pirate, so he just wears the sunglasses everywhere. He thinks it makes him look like Lou Reed."

"Well, he's not exactly wrong about that." Elise sounded shaken. She ran the pad of her thumb over the tip of the dart. "And you said you've been robbed before."

Rafferty nodded. "I don't know a driver who hasn't been."

"They don't... I mean, isn't there something you can do?"

"Like what? Fight the guy off for forty bucks? My life's worth more than that. You know bank tellers are supposed to cooperate with the robber, right? Just do what the guy says. The money is insured, and it's not yours. Don't be a hero. The class you take to be a driver, they tell you that if anyone asks how your night is going, you always say 'slow.' Busy means lucrative. Worth robbing. Otherwise, the only advice is to hand it over quick."

Elise said, "That would be horrible. Your whole night just

gone."

"I'd rather lose a night's work than an eye. Mick will be the first one to tell you he should've just handed it over. That night, he had about a hundred bucks in his pocket. A bargain considering the amount he spent on lost wages, medical bills, and sunglasses in the years since." She had retrieved her darts, but Elise still hadn't thrown. "It's your turn."

Elise stared at her darts.

Rafferty whistled. "Hey. You're going for 7 here."

"Don't get hurt."

"What?"

Elise looked up at her. "I don't know. I hadn't thought about how dangerous your job is. And now it's all I can think about."

Rafferty laughed awkwardly. "I just finished telling you about our coward policy. I don't care how much money I have in the lockbox. I'm handing it over to anyone with a knife or a gun. Or a finger in the pocket of their sweatshirt."

"Don't joke," Elise said with surprising firmness. She looked into Rafferty's eyes. "Promise me you won't get hurt."

Rafferty's smile faded as well. She wanted to say that wasn't a promise she could realistically make. But something in Elise's expression made her think twice.

"I'll do my best."

Elise nodded. "Thank you. I just..." She shook her head, looked at the dart board, and made all three of her shots in quick succession. "I like you," she said once she was done. "And I pictured you being hurt. And I didn't like it."

"I don't care much for the idea, either."

Elise laughed softly. "You must think I'm insane."

Rafferty shrugged. "I think you're intense. And I think you care about me. That's nice."

"Good." She retrieved her darts and moved out of the way.

"For the record," Rafferty said, "I like you, too."

Elise beamed.

"But that doesn't mean I won't kick your butt at this game."

Elise laughed. "Talk is cheap. Show me what you got."

Rafferty took her next shot.

CHAPTER SIX

KISSING. SOFT lips. Warm hands on her hips under her shirt. Opening her mouth, feeling someone else's tongue on hers. Pulling back to change position and seeing just a glimpse of red hair mussed from having fingers raking through it. More kissing, bodies pressed together, standing against the wall in the hallway outside her apartment. "Elise..." whispered in Rafferty's voice.

Elise gasped awake, her legs kicking at the blanket as she rolled onto her back as if she'd been physically pulled out of the dream. She was lying in her bed, alone obviously. She'd only bothered putting on a T-shirt when she got out of the bath, and now it was rucked up around her hips. She tugged it down as quickly as if she'd been exposed in public.

She looked out the open bedroom door into the rest of the apartment. The streetlight shining through the window made everything look amber. Her hair was still damp, which meant she hadn't been in bed very long. The dream must have been lurking right at the edge of her subconscious, waiting to strike. She closed her eyes and listened to her heart drumming.

Nothing like the dream had happened in real life, obviously. She and Rafferty had played a few games of darts. Then they fed some quarters into the jukebox and made fun of each other's taste in music. The bar had burgers and fries that served as their dinner.

The food was terrible, of course, but worth the convenience of not needing to leave and find somewhere else to eat.

They had talked for hours. When they finally looked around they discovered the bar had filled up and the street outside was dark.

"Guess we should call it a night."

Elise had been unable to think of an argument. "I guess so. I had fun, though."

"Me too. We're definitely doing this again."

The thrill of that, of knowing they would repeat the evening at some future unknown time, had left Elise feeling giddy for the entire ride home. She'd felt like she was walking on air as she went up to her apartment, and all through the bath. And it was more than likely why her brain had conjured the dream.

But what a dream. She never had dreams like that. So vivid and real. But at the same time, everything had been heightened. Like she was drunk, or maybe it was what being on drugs was like.

She kicked the covers out of the way and climbed out of bed, tugged at her shirt again, and went into the kitchen. She filled a glass with cold water, drank most of it, then refilled the glass and drank it all down. She hiccupped, pressed the back of her hand to her mouth, and leaned against the counter. She looked out the window at the building across the street.

She could put on clothes, go down the street to the payphone, and call Michael again. Even as she had the thought, she hated herself for it. She hated thinking of him as a lifeline. She needed to forget his number. Whatever she was going through, there was nothing he could do to help. Even if she was willing to explain the situation to him, which she absolutely was *not*.

Another idea occurred to her. She went to the bedroom and put on pants, then buttoned a shirt over her T-shirt. She didn't bother fixing her hair, instead hiding it under a baseball cap that she pulled low on her forehead like she was trying to sneak past a warden. She left her apartment and speed-walked to the payphone. She didn't call Michael, instead choosing a number that she'd avoiding using since she came to the city.

Despite the hour, her call was answered on the third ring. "Hello."

Just the sound of his voice made her smile. "Hi, Vic. It's Elise Herald."

He laughed. "Land alive! Oh my goodness. I hope you're in

another time zone, considering the hour it is. But I'll forgive you for being rude if it means you're close enough to drop by."

"Sorry about that, Vic. But I *am* in town. And I'm calling because I wanted to come over for a special screening, if that's okay."

"Of course, of course. You know me. A nap at sunrise and a nap at sunset, and I'm pretty much set for the day. Tell me what you're in the mood for and I'll have it set up when you get here."

"I don't care. Something funny and romantic. Something from the fifties or sixties."

"Ah, dealer's choice. I'll find something perfect for you."

She smiled. "Thanks, Vic. I owe you."

"Not a dime, Leese. I'll see you soon."

She confirmed his address before she hung up. Her plan had been to take the train, but a cab happened to be passing by just as she reached the curb. The headlights blinded her too much to see who was driving, but she took a risk and raised her arm. It slowed and pulled to the curb, where she saw the logo on the door was for one of Achilles' rivals. It felt wrong to give money to a different company. But at the same time, she was grateful. This meant she wouldn't run into a coworker.

Elise gave the address as she climbed into the backseat. Once she was buckled in, the driver pulled away from the curb and set out.

"So how's your night going?" she asked.

"Slow," the driver said.

Elise laughed so hard that he probably thought she was insane, but she didn't even try to stop or apologize for finding it hilarious.

Vic gave her a wide elfin smile as he swung open the door. She remembered him being a giant of a man, but she'd grown and he'd become a little hunched over in the years since she'd last visited. "Leese!" He laughed and stepped outside to hug her, then pulled her over the threshold into his home. "Look at you. I haven't seen you in a decade or more. How are your parents?"

"They're fine, Vic. And... a-and if you could maybe not mention this visit to them..."

He raised his eyebrows at her. "Secrets? Is everything okay?"

"Everything's fine. I just need to not be... findable. For a little while."

"Okay." He put a hand on his chest and lowered his chin as if taking an oath. "If they ask, I'll tell them you're safe and healthy. Or seem safe and healthy." He narrowed his eyes. "Are~"

"I am safe and healthy," she said with a laugh.

"Then I shall tell them that and nothing else. You're an adult." He clapped his hands together and looked down the narrow hall behind him. "Now. It's all set up and ready. Do you like Miss Grace Kelly?"

"She's only my very favorite."

He grinned. "Then you will be very pleased!" He gestured down the hall. "Go on. Have a seat. I'll get the movie started. Do you want any snacks? Something to drink?"

"No, thank you, Vic. The movie is exactly what I need." She took out her wallet. "I only have a couple of singles~"

His brows lowered and he fixed her with a comically angry glare. "Money? *Money?* I offer you love and you turn it into a transaction. The audacity."

"It would make me feel better."

He put a hand on top of hers and pushed the wallet down. "Next time. *If* you get candy."

"Fair enough." She bent down and kissed his cheek. "Thank you."

"Ah, you're doing me the favor." The glee returned to his face. "Living out my fantasy of running a bootleg movie theater. I'm going to feel like a criminal for the rest of the week!" He laughed and did a quick jig. "Go on, I just have to go get the projector running."

She watched him go, then went down the hall. The room at the end had been converted into a dollhouse version of a movie theater. It couldn't seat more than a dozen people, but she doubted it had ever been anywhere close to capacity. Vic had been collecting old movie reels his entire life and took great joy in holding private shows for friends and family. He projected the films directly onto the far wall from a cut-out that led into his "projector room."

Elise took a seat in the middle of the room. The chairs were plush and easy to sink into. He never charged, but sometimes people felt obligated to leave a donation. He spent the money on improvements to the theater. He made sure his apartment was always well-stocked with candy and bags of Jiffy Pop, and he was always improving the seats.

The wall ahead of her came to life with a rectangle of flickering light. She smiled and settled back, tucking her legs up under her.

She was awake long enough to see the title card - *High Society*, an old favorite - but she was asleep before the first song ended.

Rafferty slipped into the backseat of the cab. "Just drive."

Tim Kuberski took the cigar from his mouth with one hand, using the other to spin the wheel. "You know, I've been waiting my whole career to have someone jump into the back of my cab and say 'just drive' or 'follow that car.' It finally happens, and it's you."

She rolled her eyes. "Fine." She pointed over the seat at a pair of taillights ahead of them. "Follow that car. And there's an extra sawbuck in it if you're not spotted."

"Moneybags over here."

"What? How much is a sawbuck?"

"Ten."

"Screw that." She dropped back into the seat and crossed her arms. "You'll get a nice tip. If you're lucky."

He grunted and stuck the cigar back in his mouth. "So what was the big emergency that you had to call and request me personally?"

She sighed and looked out the window. "I needed to talk to someone. And I didn't want to do it in the garage where Frank or Bob could overhear."

He looked at her in the rearview. "Everything okay?"

"I don't know. Maybe. I went out with someone tonight. Not a date. It wasn't a date. It was *not* a date. But it kind of felt like a date. Sometimes."

"What did you do on this not-date get-together?"

"Played pool, drank, played darts. Talked."

He shrugged. "I've had worse dates. And better times just hanging out. Did you get a goodnight kiss at the end of the night?"

"No," she said.

"Had a lot of dates like that, too," he muttered. "Okay. So it could go either way. Could be just two friends spending time together, it could've been a date. You're straight down the middle. The only thing that matters is how you feel about him."

"Her," Rafferty said.

He grunted. "Who her?"

She sighed. "Her that we've been talking about, her that I went out with. It's a *her*, Tim, because I'm gay, which I've told you three or four times by this point."

"Oh, right, right. The guys never talk about it at the garage."

"Which is why you're the only one I've told."

Tim nodded. "Okay, so *her*. This *her* girl you went out with. The definition of what it was comes from how you feel about her. Do you *feel* like it was a date?"

Rafferty looked out the window. "I hope it was..."

"Well, there you go. Now you just have to ask her what it was~"

"Absolutely not. No." She shook her head.

Tim said, "Then tell *her* what *you* think it was. It sounds to me like you're expecting her to be a mind-reader. Just be honest with the lady."

"But if I do that," Rafferty said, "and she *doesn't* think it was a date, it would be insanely awkward between us. I would rather just have ambiguous hangouts with her than nothing. If she knows I have feelings for her - if I can even call them that after one maybe-not-a-date-at-all - it might make her hold off on agreeing to going out again."

"You've got to take the risk if you're going to get anywhere, Raff." He looked down at his watch. "Do you really not care where we go? Because I haven't had my break yet, and I'm dying for a hot dog."

"Sure." She dropped back again, unsure when she had even slid to the edge of the seat this time. "I'll even pay for it. Cheaper than a therapist."

Tim laughed. "You get what you pay for, Raff."

She smiled and closed her eyes.

It would be lovely and wonderful if Elise felt the same way about her. But it was also lovely and wonderful to have her as a friend. At the moment it didn't seem possible to test the waters without threatening what they already had. Going to the laundromat together. Spending their nights off hustling each other at pool and darts.

Laundry and darts. She could be very happy with that.

CHAPTER SEVEN

THEY KEPT up their routine over the next week and a half. Rafferty started spending time in the maintenance part of the garage before and after her shifts. She only ended up at the card table with the guys when Elise was too busy with work. One night while she was playing poker with the guys, Hugh and Frank got up to get snacks from the vending machine and left her sitting alone with Tim. He checked to make sure the others weren't in earshot before he took out his cigar and held it so his mouth was covered.

"Her, huh?"

"What's that?" Rafferty said.

He raised a bushy eyebrow and leaned in closer. "*He-e-er*." He glanced over his shoulder to the spot where Elise was washing Cab 701. "From our talk. Her is her."

Rafferty shrugged. "I don't know what you're talking about."

He chuckled and bit down on the end of his cigar again. "Sure, sure. You could do a lot worse." He rearranged his cards. "She couldn't. But you definitely could."

She threw a pretzel in his face.

That night, when she got back to the garage, Elise was waiting for her by the lockers. Rafferty smiled at the sight of her even as she chided herself for acting like a teenager.

"You lurk around lockers?" she asked. "What is this, high

school?"

"Please, I didn't have the nerve to hang around lockers in high school." Elise leaned against the bank of lockers, her hands folded in front of her. "So, um. About driving me home…"

Rafferty tossed her cap into her locker and retrieved her personal car keys. "Did you make other arrangements?" she guessed. "Or are you pulling a double?"

"No, nothing like that. I'd still like a ride home if you're willing. But there's something I want to show you instead of going straight home. Or I guess 'share with you' would be more accurate. Would that be okay?"

"Uh, sure. I don't have any plans after work. What did you have in mind?"

"It's really more of a show thing, not a tell thing."

Rafferty nodded. "Okay. You have me intrigued."

"Great. I'll be right back."

Elise's smile was enough to make Rafferty agree to anything. She had no idea how she could've fallen so far, so fast. She closed her locker and headed down to wait for Elise in the parking lot. Even with the security fence and the yellow-brown halo of the security light, she checked the corners and shadowed parts of the lot for anyone who might be lying in wait. She could smell the Hudson, the wind coming off of it just chilly enough to make her wish she'd brought a jacket.

When Elise returned, she had traded her blue coveralls for a white button-down and jeans. Rafferty refused to make a comment about how good she looked, but the thought was too loud for her to silence it inside her head.

"So where am I headed?" Rafferty asked as she got behind the wheel.

Elise made a face. "I should probably warn you that what I have in mind is going to take maybe two hours. I should've mentioned that before you agreed to anything."

Rafferty shrugged. "I usually spend a few hours after work wandering around my apartment anyway."

"Okay." Elise sighed with relief and fastened her seatbelt. "In that case, 44th and Eighth."

"Do I get to know what's waiting for us there?"

Elise considered the question for longer than Rafferty thought was necessary. Finally she said, "No. I want it to be a surprise."

Rafferty was very curious what kind of surprise could be

waiting at four in the morning, but she was willing to go along with it.

"It wasn't that long ago you didn't even know where to eat," Rafferty pointed out. "Now you have *secrets*."

Elise just laughed. "I knew about this place back then. It just wasn't, um... I just... I didn't know you very well yet."

"Oh," Rafferty said, hoping she wasn't blushing. "Okay, then."

As she drove south, Elise reached up and untied her ponytail, dropping her head forward to rake through the hair with both hands. It fell loose on her shoulders when she was finished, and she sighed and settled back in her seat.

"Feels good to get out of the garage," she said.

Rafferty didn't feel like that required a response, so she kept silent as she turned onto West 44th. Any comment she would have made would be about how pretty Elise's hair looked down, and she definitely didn't want to say that. She inhaled deeply and let the air out as slowly as she could.

"Are you okay?"

"Hm? Yeah. Fine."

"You just sighed really heavily. If you'd rather just take me home, that's~"

"No, no. It's not you. Honest." She smiled. "I'm excited about the surprise. I'm just..." She gestured at the road ahead. "I'm sick of driving. After twelve hours it gets dull."

Elise said, "Oh! Oh, I can imagine."

When Rafferty turned onto 44th, Elise started scanning for parking spots. "Anywhere around here is good. We can walk from here. It's not far."

Rafferty did a quick scan for signs that listed parking restrictions out of habit, then pulled to the curb. Elise got out and moved with more speed than anyone who had just finished a twelve-hour shift should've been capable of, turning only once to make sure Rafferty was keeping up.

None of the businesses along the street were open at this hour but she scanned the darkened windows. Restaurants, a spa, a barber shop... there was a tavern, but even that was closed. It wasn't exactly the sort of seedy establishments she expected to encounter at this time of night, and the fact that the upper floors seemed to be fairly tidy residential apartments made it even more intriguing.

"I *love* this time of night," Elise said. "It's so quiet. And everything is closed. It's like the world got turned off, but we're still sneaking around in it."

"I get that feeling," Rafferty said.

"You do?" Elise closed the distance between them. "Do you ever feel like you're the only real person in the world? Like, how can *all* these other people have the same experience you do? The same life, the same long days." She looked around. "Times like this, it makes sense. I'm the only one who is real and the world is for me, and everyone else is just background actors."

Rafferty chuckled. "I don't get that feeling. No. I wish I did. It sounds kind of fun."

Elise chuckled. "It is. It makes it easy to stop worrying about what people think of you. How you dress, if you trip on a curb, if your hair isn't done. If I could just flip a switch and be like that all the time..."

"I think what you're thinking of turning off is called 'empathy,' and turned it off would be a very bad thing."

Elise laughed again, then covered her mouth. "God. You're right. That would be bad."

"Right now it's not bad. Right now it's probably okay to think you're the only person in the world."

She looked at Elise, who looked back at her. In the dark, staring silently at each other, it seemed like something was passing between them. Rafferty instinctively wanted to look away, but she also wanted to keep staring until she figured out exactly what shade of blue Elise's eyes were. They were different in the near-dark. Like water.

"Yeah," Elise said softly.

"Was this what you wanted to share with me?"

Elise blinked, breaking the spell. "Oh! No."

She grabbed Rafferty's hand, setting off again. Rafferty allowed herself to be dragged a little further down the street. Elise stopped in front of a wrought-iron fence around stairs that led down to a small, undecorated stoop below street level. Rafferty looked down at the unmarked doorway and then back at Elise.

"Should I have told Mick I was leaving with you...?"

Elise rolled her eyes and hooked her arm around Rafferty's. "Come on. It's going to be fun. I promise."

Rafferty followed her down the steps. Elise knocked and took a step back, then pulled out her wallet. She tried to angle it so she could see, but the moon and streetlights didn't reach far enough to help her out. She took out a bill and squinted at it.

"Shoot. Is this a one or a five?"

The door opened before Rafferty could answer. A lamp inside provided enough light that they could both see she was holding a wrinkled one dollar bill. The man who had answered the knock was a full head shorter than both of them with a shockingly thick Brillo pad of white hair. He was dressed in a sweater and khakis despite the hour. He looked at the money in Elise's hand, scowled, and then lifted his eyes to examine Rafferty for a long moment.

Finally he looked at Elise fully. The scowl was gone, replaced by a friendly, almost grandfatherly smile. "What will it be tonight, love?"

"*The Heist*, if it's handy." She held out the dollar. "I'm getting candy this time!"

He sighed and seemed to surrender. He folded his hand around the bill and vanished it into a pocket. Then he stepped to one side and ushered them inside.

The small foyer had barely enough room for all three of them. The red carpet was so thick that Rafferty felt like she was sinking into it as the old man opened a cabinet and withdrew a wide, narrow box that he turned and held it out to them. It was full of candy. Twix bars, Snickers, Laffy Taffy, Pop Rocks, wax bottles... Elise took two sleeves of Reese's cups and looked at Rafferty, who chose a small bag of Jelly Belly.

The man nodded as if approving of their choices, then returned the tray to the cupboard. Without turning, he gestured to one of the two doors in the foyer.

"You know the way," he said.

"Thanks, Vic." To Rafferty, under her breath, she said, "Come on."

Rafferty watched Vic disappear through the other door. She followed Elise into a dark hallway and put a hand on her arm.

"Is this illegal? I'm not opposed, I just want to know if I should be ready to run."

"Not illegal," Elise laughed. "I promise."

Rafferty decided to take her at her word. The hallway was short and led into a room that was empty except for five rows of seats, four seats to each row, facing a blank wall. There was a square cut into the back wall and, through it, Rafferty saw a large machine with a glass lens on the front. Someone, she presumed it was Vic, moved around in the room behind the contraption as Elise walked to the middle row and chose a seat.

"Is this a movie theater?" Rafferty asked.

"Only in the barest definition of the word," Elise said. "Vic's an old friend. He has a whole library of old, old movies and he holds screenings for people."

Rafferty took a seat next to Elise. "At four in the morning?"

"Whenever people want to come," Elise said with a shrug. "I came and watched a movie the other night. I thought about inviting you but I chickened out. I finally decided that I wanted you to know about it. I wanted to share it with you. Thanks for agreeing to come with me."

"Sure. What movie did you say it was? *The Heist!* I don't think I've heard of that one."

"It's from 1952. Do you know Evelyn Wade?" Rafferty tried to place the name, but finally shook her head. "She was going to be the next big thing for a while in the forties. But she chose to stand up against sexism and the general asshole-ness of the industry and took a bit of a tumble. She still got a lot of work, and she was recognized, but it was rough for a while."

The lights dimmed and the projector began to emit a low hum. Rafferty watched as a rectangle of light appeared on the wall in front of them.

"She had a good career. Not amazing. But decent enough. She wasn't an Audrey Hepburn but people knew who she was."

The film started and, a second later, the audio came through speakers that Rafferty couldn't see. The title - THE HEIST! - appeared in big yellow letters against a pale blue background. As the credits rolled, Elise opened her candy bar. Rafferty decided to open her candy as well.

"She was married to a reporter named Simon Grace. He wasn't really famous at all outside of local papers, but he made a decent living. He died about a year ago. And that's when the big secret came out." She let the theme music of the movie play, building the tension. "Turns out Simon Grace was really Grace Simon. She'd been living as a man for most of her adult life. Evelyn admitted it before the scandal rags could get their mitts on it. Her agent shushed it up, otherwise it would've been a whole thing. It got buried quick. No one really cared about a scandal that involved a barely-known actress from thirty years ago. I only saw it because I was already a big fan of her."

Rafferty was shocked she hadn't heard anything about it. The movie had begun, and a posh-looking woman was walking down a

New York street.

"That's her," Elise whispered. "That's Evelyn Wade."

She was gorgeous. The colors were overly vibrant so the blue of her eyes and the blonde of her hair popped unnaturally against Vic's plain wall. Rafferty watched as she walked into a jewelry shop and began arguing with the clerk almost immediately. All she could think about was the fact this woman, in her real life, was a lesbian. She had a wife at home, a partner who dressed as a man and used a different name outside of their house.

"When I found out she was gay, it was like I was looking at a mirror and all of a sudden it turned into a window. She looked the same. But knowing she had that secret... she had it then, while she was filming this, it made me think about a lot of things. It made me think about how I might have been keeping secrets from myself."

Rafferty was staring at Elise now, not even bothering to look at the movie.

"I liked Evelyn Wade, because she reminded me of myself. We looked similar, sure." She chuckled and shrugged. "And then there was this new fact about it. And it made sense. It fit. And I couldn't help but wonder if maybe that piece, that secret, had been what I was sensing the whole time. Suddenly I thought maybe we had a lot more in common than just our hair color."

She looked at Rafferty and seemed to be surprised she was staring at her. She quickly looked away, back at the screen.

"This, um, this movie... She made this right after she married Gracie. She and Betty Gallagher play two women who accidentally steal a priceless diamond. They have to run from the jeweler, the cops, and the mafia, trying to get it back where it belongs without ending up in prison for theft. It's goofy and slapstick, but it's one of the earliest movies with two women as the headliners. I always loved it. She and Betty had such good chemistry..."

Rafferty looked at the flickering images again. Evelyn and another woman, probably Betty Gallagher, were arguing in an alleyway. Betty walloped Evelyn with her purse. Evelyn's eyes bugged out and she reared back one fist as if she was going to punch Betty's lights out.

"It was a romance without the kissing," Elise said. "The movie ends with them sitting together in a dumpster, hugging and laughing as trash gets dumped on their heads. Oh. Uh, sorry for ruining the ending."

"That's okay," Rafferty said. "I'll act surprised."

Elise was still staring up at the movie. She was silent long enough for the two characters to have a long, passionate argument which ended with them nose-to-nose, teeth bared.

"I wanted them to kiss," Elise said under her breath. "I watched it again after I found out the truth about Evelyn. And I realized that more than anything, I had always wanted them to kiss."

Rafferty shifted uncomfortably in her chair. "We never talked about that book you loaned me."

"No," Elise said. "We didn't."

"I didn't know what to say. If you wanted me to say anything, if you *expected* me to say anything. So I just didn't say anything. Which you probably took as a signal."

Elise nodded. "I did."

"I'm sorry."

"You don't have to be sorry. I'm just glad it didn't scare you away from spending time with me."

"If anything it made me want to spend more time with you."

Elise smiled. "Good. Anyway, this movie, and the story I told you about Evelyn Wade, I wanted to be sure you knew that I was like her."

"Oh." Rafferty felt like something of importance needed to be said, some kind of acknowledgement or affirmation. She wasn't good at being that person. She never knew what to say or how to make someone else feel better. Everything she considered seemed trite or unworthy of what Elise had just confessed to her. And she knew that the longer she sat there without doing anything, the worse it would be. Elise had laid herself bare and it deserved some response.

She reached out and slid her hand over the back of Elise's. Elise looked down, looked at Rafferty, then turned her wrist so their palms lined up. Rafferty slipped her fingers between Elise's and squeezed gently.

Elise squeezed back. "Thank you."

Rafferty nodded. "Thank you for telling me that."

Elise smiled and looked up at the movie again. "It really is a good movie."

"Okay. Thanks for bringing me."

"Sure."

Rafferty settled into her seat and looked up at the film. Evelyn and Betty were still arguing. She had to admit, Elise definitely had a point about their chemistry. She glanced down at their joined fingers without moving her head. Elise didn't seem eager to let go, and Rafferty decided she didn't mind it much herself. She decided to just enjoy the movie. And, despite Elise spilling the beans about how it ended, she was still going to hope it ended with a kiss.

Chapter Eight

IT WAS just after dawn when they finally left Vic's theater. The rest of the city was just starting to wake up. Rafferty offered to buy Elise breakfast, which Elise gratefully accepted, and they drove to a diner near Elise's apartment. She got oatmeal with banana slices and Elise got scrambled eggs with bacon.

"I'm still not used to breakfast foods right before bed." She squinted out the front window of the diner, where the rising sun was streaming down the street. "Or trying to go to sleep while it's still so bright outside."

"Blackout curtains," Rafferty said. "They're life-changing."

"I have them. But if you get up to use the bathroom, it's hard to adjust."

Rafferty nodded. "That's true. But I wouldn't trade night shift for anything. I like the quiet. It's the only time Manhattan ever gets that quiet. It's nice."

Elise said, "The quiet is definitely nice. Couldn't you make more money if you worked days, though?"

"It's a crapshoot," Rafferty said, shrugging. "Working the day means a lot more Wall Street douchebags, tourists, people heading off to lunch meetings. The traffic is also much crazier, which makes the passengers more irritable, which only makes things more stressful. You get more hookers and strippers on night shift, but they're almost always polite, friendly, and they tip very well. And I like the way they always look relieved when they realize they have a woman driving them."

"I bet that's a wonderful feeling," Elise said. "You're their safe space."

Rafferty felt suddenly bashful. "Yeah. It does feel pretty great knowing someone, even a stranger, can relax because you're there."

Elise said, "Well, you're definitely a safe place for me. This is a big scary city and you make it feel less imposing."

"I'm... I'm glad," Rafferty said, then chuckled awkwardly. "Sorry. I'm not sure how to react to someone saying I make them feel safe. I'm honored, though."

They ate quietly for a bit, letting the hum of conversation around them fill the silence. When they finished eating, they argued briefly over who would pay. They eventually settled on Rafferty paying the bill while Elise left a tip for the waitress. Elise said they would switch next time, and the idea of making this a regular occurrence gave Rafferty butterflies that she hadn't been expecting.

She drove Elise home and, when she pulled to the curb, Elise didn't reach to unfasten her seatbelt. She just stared straight ahead, one hand on her thigh and the other resting on the rolled-down window. Rafferty waited for her to say something, to explain what she was waiting for, but she kept her lips pressed together and jaw set tight.

"Well," Rafferty said. "It's been a long day.."

"Uh-huh." Elise snapped out of whatever daydream she'd been caught up in. "I was just... Right." She unfastened her seatbelt and reached for the door handle. She dropped her hand again. "Do you want to come upstairs?"

"Up...?" Rafferty didn't bother acting like she didn't know what Elise meant. "Oh. I'm not sure that would be a good idea."

Elise finally looked at her. "God, I'm not jumping to conclusions, am I? I am. I just assumed you were gay. I don't know why." She flinched away and covered her eyes. "I'm such an imbecile."

"You're not an imbecile," Rafferty said. "You're right about me. And I think you're incredibly attractive. I want to say yes. I think going upstairs would be a very interesting turn and I'd like to see where it goes."

"Really?"

"Really. But I can't. Or I could, but I won't." Now it was

Rafferty's turn to stare awkwardly ahead. "You deserve to keep your secrets. You don't have to tell me anything about where you came from or what you left behind. You didn't say you left someone behind. And maybe you didn't. Maybe you were single when you left. But I don't think so. Something about the way you talk about it..."

Her voice trailed off. They both stared at spots that the other person wasn't, desperate to avoid accidental eye contact.

"Like I said," Rafferty continued after a few seconds, "maybe I'm wrong. I don't have any evidence to back it up. And you don't have to tell me anything about anything. But if I'm going to go upstairs with you, I need to know there's not someone waiting for you to come home to them."

Elise didn't say anything for a long time. People walked past them on the way to work, ignoring the tension that Rafferty thought had to be emanating from the car like a heat bubble.

"I can't tell you that," Elise finally said.

"Okay," Rafferty said.

"I'm not married," Elise added.

"Okay," Rafferty said again.

"But I'd be lying if I said I was free and clear."

Rafferty moved her hand to the top of the steering wheel. "I get that. I don't need the details. But that's enough to keep me from going upstairs with you right now."

"I understand. That's the right reaction, honestly." She looked down at her hands. "So I'm just going to go."

"Sleep well."

"You too. I'll see you tomo~ well, this afternoon, I guess. Will you still give me a ride home after our shift?"

Rafferty was surprised she had to ask. "Sure. Just because..." She didn't finish the thought. "Yeah. I'll bring you home."

"Okay. Thank you, Rafferty."

"You can call me Raff if you want."

Elise smiled. "Really? What about Sally?"

"Never."

Elise laughed, which helped defuse the tension. "I can deal with that. Good night, Raff."

"Night."

Even though the sun was up, she still waited until Elise was inside before she left. She also waited until she was a block away to press the heel of her hand against her face and slap one cheek, then the other. She knew she'd absolutely made the right decision. Hell, it wasn't even a decision in her books. If Elise was engaged to someone before she came to New York, if she was even just dating someone, Rafferty wouldn't be part to adultery.

But saying no to Elise's invitation, especially out of respect for a relationship that was entirely hypothetical from Rafferty's point of view, had been really fucking hard.

Morality was its own reward, and the prize for it was she got to keep thinking of herself as a good person. She tried to be okay with that. She spent the whole drive home trying to tell herself that denying herself to protect a relationship that Elise had run away and changed her entire life to escape was a good deed.

She was still trying when she changed for bed, and even as she fell asleep trying not to think about alternate realities where she was a slightly worse, slightly more selfish kind of person.

Elise wanted to run to the payphone and call Michael immediately. But it was too late in the day, and she was worried he would hear the street noise and figure out where she was. Did traffic in Manhattan have a unique sound? Would someone walking by on the sidewalk shout out a specific address at the exact wrong time? She couldn't risk it. She was already taking a chance he might contact the phone company and figure out the area code where the calls were coming from. She couldn't give him another clue.

So instead she took off her clothes to prevent any spur of the moment decisions. She couldn't leave the apartment naked, no matter what her brain tried to tell her. And since she was already naked, she ran a bath and sank into it. Couldn't leave the apartment if she was naked *and* wet. She'd likely be arrested before she got anywhere near the phone booth.

She wished she had just lied. The relationship *was* over, just maybe not officially. It was just missing the official death certificate, something she could create with a simple phone call.

Okay. Maybe it wouldn't be a *simple* phone call. But there was no chance of a reconciliation. She wasn't going back to Saratoga Springs. She would never go back to Michael. Did she want to risk missing her chance with Rafferty because she refused to finally pull the trigger on what she left behind?

Elise didn't even know what would have happened if Rafferty had agreed to come up. She hadn't thought beyond the invitation. She hadn't so much as kissed another woman, and maybe Rafferty would have been fine with stopping there. But what if she expected more? Elise didn't know if she would have been ready for that, or strong enough to stop things before they went too far. In retrospect, asking Rafferty up had been a very bad idea, and she was grateful Rafferty had done the right thing and said no.

So why did she feel so utterly rejected?

She cupped her hands under the water and dumped them over her head, then ran her fingers through her hair.

"You are one supremely messed-up human being, Elise Herald."

She thought it was a flaw of human programming that she could be keenly aware of that fact and yet, apparently, powerless to change it.

On Halloween night, Achilles Cab Company had an arrangement with a local law firm. People too drunk to get themselves home could call a special number, and a cab would show up to take them home for free. Drivers kept track of the fare, reported it to Mick, and he passed it on to the firm. They would then pay the fees, and Mick would pay the cabbies what they were owed. They ran the same deal on New Years Eve, and drivers were assigned on a volunteer basis.

Rafferty appreciated the idea of the set-up, but all the drivers hated it. Firstly because instead of driving around looking for fares, the designated driver had to wait around for calls to come in. Sometimes there were a handful of calls to take care of. One year, Frank reported that he'd spent the entire night hanging out in the garage for one lousy call at two-thirty in the morning. He'd made a grand total of eight dollars that night.

And even when the designated shift was busy, they didn't get a dime until the paperwork was all filed. Sometimes it could take up to two weeks before they actually had the cash in hand. Not everyone could afford to wait that long to get paid, which meant most years Mick had to offer incentives. Tonight, it was the fact that Cab 521 - the figurative Rolls Royce of the Achilles fleet - was the designated car for the free rides. It was new, it rode smooth, and it was a joy to drive compared to some of the other cabs. When no one stepped forward, he added a ten percent boost to all fares on her next regular shift, money she could keep rather than paying to him and the Reverend.

Rafferty finally took pity on the poor man and stepped forward to take the fall. The other drivers were so grateful that Tim suggested a "Halloween pool" in which everyone set aside fifteen dollars of whatever they brought in for her. Rafferty gratefully accepted. It wouldn't be the best night she'd ever had, but it definitely took some of the sting out of waiting around all night.

She arrived on Halloween dressed in a baseball uniform, her hair done in braids. Elise saw her coming down the ramp and smiled at her costume.

"Who are you supposed to be?"

"Caroline Rainey, one of the first female pitchers in the MLB." She turned around to reveal the name on her back of her jersey. "A personal hero."

Elise said, "Very nice. I think I had her baseball card." She looked Rafferty up and down again, then nodded. "You look good."

"Thanks," Rafferty said.

The rest of the drivers on the graveyard shift had also dressed up. A few years ago, Bob decided to dress up as a mummy for the Halloween shift. A group of partiers had given him a fifty dollar tip because it had been "just perfect" to be driven by a monster. Once word got out, it quickly became tradition. Hugh and Tim had asked multiple times to actually decorate the cabs, but Mick firmly put his foot down on that.

On this Halloween, Rafferty thought everyone had gone above and beyond. Frank hadn't shaved for a few days, center-parted his hair, and was wearing a torn plaid shirt over a T-shirt. He claimed that made him a werewolf. Hugh was dressed as a ghostbuster, which was basically a jumpsuit with a logo drawn on the shoulder. Rafferty hadn't seen the movie but she thought it was fairly accurate. Tim was Spock, from *Star Trek*, and Bob was a Stormtrooper from *Star Wars*. They were playing cards together, and Bob sadly informed her that Mick refused to let him wear his helmet while on duty.

"I'm sure your passengers will appreciate that, Bob," Rafferty said as they dealt her in. She glanced around to see if Elise wanted to play, but she had disappeared.

The game fell apart as the day shift came in and cabs became available. Frank went first, followed by Bob, Hugh, Tim, and Doc, which finally left Rafferty on her own at the table. She gathered the cards and set up a game of Solitaire. It was much too early to expect any calls, but the deal with the law firm insisted on having a driver available for the entire overnight shift. Rafferty didn't understand the logic of having someone on stand-by before most bars were even open, but she would suffer so everyone else could thrive.

She got bored after two games of cards. She refused to look at the clock to see how little time had passed. She knew it would only make the night feel endless. She looked around the garage and considered the Frogger game in the corner, but she didn't have any quarters. She twisted to look at the row of cabs awaiting maintenance. Cab 211 was jacked up a little ways off the floor, and a pair of coveralled legs sticking out from underneath one of them. Elise's knees were bent, her feet flat on the floor, and the rest of her was under the chassis. She looked like the Wicked Witch of the East from *Wizard of Oz*.

Rafferty got up and walked over, bending at the waist to try peeking under the car. She bumped Elise's work boot.

"Hey. Got room for one more under there?"

"Sure! Pull up a sled."

Rafferty looked and spotted a long red board with wheels. She laid down on it and, after a few attempts, figured out how to use her feet to steer it under the cab. She was surprisingly anxious about actually going under the car, very aware of how heavy it was and how thin the jacks holding it up were. Elise had scooted her sled to one side to give her room, and now both their legs were sticking out from under the front bumper. It probably looked like a horrible rush hour accident.

"Are these really called sleds?" Rafferty asked.

"I think they're called creepers," Elise said. "But I don't like how that sounds. Sled fits better." She pushed herself up, then back down, then lined herself up with Rafferty again. "It's fun."

"And the jacks are sturdy?"

Elise said, "Well, fairly." She looked at Rafferty and laughed. "Oh, god, I'm sorry. Yes. They're sturdy. You don't have to worry. We're safe."

"If you say so." Rafferty looked up at the undercarriage of the cab. "You know, as many of these as I've been in, I don't think I've ever seen what's under here. You actually know what all this stuff is?"

"Sure." Elise pointed. "That, for instance, is your front timber suspension axle."

Rafferty stared at the long metal rod. "See, you're fucking with me, and it's not working because for all I know you're telling the truth."

Elise laughed. "It's okay. You don't need to know all this stuff. You have me for all that."

"What made you want to learn about cars?"

"Had to do something," Elise said. "And I didn't like horses."

Rafferty frowned. "Horses?"

Elise smiled and declined to elaborate. "It's probably like you deciding to drive a cab. You can't really explain it. You just understand what you like without analyzing it." She put down a tool and lifted her head to search for another. "Cars are constant problems. You can get one running smoothly, everything perfect, and then suddenly there's a rattle or a clunking noise or a squeak. Then you find the problem, you fix the problem. Easy. Life has too many problems you can't just track down and fix. I like cars because they're simple."

"That makes sense," Rafferty said. "Do you really not like horses?"

Elise laughed. "They're fine."

Rafferty folded her hands on her stomach and watched Elise work. In the silence, it was easier to notice they were laying side-by-side, shoulders touching, very much like they were in bed together. She tensed at the thought.

"It's a good thing you're doing," Elise said. "Sacrificing your income to make sure people have a safe way to get home."

"It's not a huge sacrifice. The guys are helping out."

"Still," Elise said. "You may have helped save some lives tonight. I'm proud of you for stepping up."

"Well, if *you're* proud of me, that's enough."

Elise grinned up at the undercarriage of the cab. "Raff. About what we discussed at breakfast. About, you know, where I came from and..."

"Yeah," Rafferty didn't want her to go into too much detail, even if no one else was in the garage to eavesdrop. "I know what you're talking about."

"I want you to know I'm trying. I haven't done it yet. There's a lot of..." She pressed her lips together, then finally turned her head to look at Rafferty. "I'm trying."

"I understand."

The intercom squealed and buzzed to life. "Rafferty! I got one for you."

Rafferty reluctantly looked away from Elise to check her watch. "Who the hell is getting drunk enough to need a sober ride at five-thirty in the afternoon?"

"Thank God for raging alcoholics," Elise said, then reached out and took Rafferty's hand. She turned it to see the watch face. "This is great. I love this. It's so big and clunky. In a good way."

"Yeah." Rafferty tried not to think too hard about Elise's hand in hers. "I like the weight of it. You've seen it before. I showed you the first day you worked here."

"Oh did you?" Elise finally let her go. "I guess I forgot. Lots of new stuff that day. Not all of it stuck in the brain."

"Uh huh," Rafferty said.

"*Rafferty*," Mick said again. "Where you at?"

"I don't know how to reverse. Give me a push."

Elise laughed and put her hand on Rafferty's shoulder. "Lift your feet."

She pushed, and Rafferty awkwardly rolled out from under the cab. She sat up off the sled too fast, giving herself a head rush. She took a second to get reoriented, then went to get the keys to her cab.

CHAPTER NINE

THERE WAS an enormous flaw in the sober driving plan. It wasn't a flaw the lawyers, the cab company, or drivers could have done much about. Rafferty discovered it on her third call of the night. It was a little after one in the morning. A vampire and a pirate were waiting on the curb outside the bar that had made the call. She pulled over to the curb and leaned across the seat to roll down the passenger side window. She whistled to get their attention.

"You guys need a cab?"

"We don't have any cash."

"It's a sober ride program," she explained for the third time of the night. "The bartender just wants to make sure you get home safe. You don't have to pay."

Pirate slurred, "That sounds like a trap. Don't get in this lady's car, man."

Vampire groaned, his head lolling forward like his neck had been turned to rubber.

"Come on, fellas," she said. "It's cold and you have to figure out a way to get home eventually. You might as well get in. I don't have all night." The last part was a complete lie. But she didn't want to spend a second more than necessary talking to these guys.

Pirate grunted and bumped Vampire's arm. "I think she's legit.

Okay. Let's go."

It took them a full minute to get to their feet. Rafferty got out of the cab and went around to the passenger side to help them as much as she could.

"Where are you guys heading?" she asked.

"Home."

She bit back a slew of swear words. "I'm going to need an address, friend."

"Oh. Right. Yeah. Okay."

Vampire got into the backseat and scooted to the far side. He rested his face against the glass of the window and seemed to fall asleep. Pirate stumbled and almost fell backward, but Rafferty caught him. To do it, though, she had to step one foot off the curb. She had one hand on his shoulder and the other on his chest. He swayed against her. She could tell that he was heavy enough that she would be trapped if he fell on top of her.

"You okay?" she asked.

"Mm-hmm," he said. "Just trying to remember..." He drew in the air with one finger. "Numbers. House numbers. Oh! My wallet!"

Rafferty nodded. "Yeah, check your license. That's gotta have your address on it."

He fumbled in his pocket. Rafferty kept him propped up, one foot on the street between the curb and the cab. She bent down to look at Vampire.

"Don't you dare puke in my cab, Nosferatu. Same goes for you, pirate-man. If you feel queasy, I'll pull over. But don't~"

She didn't have a chance to finish the threat, because that was the moment the flaw in the sober driving program became extremely relevant. For every person who was responsible and called for a designated driver, there were a hundred others who decided they were fine to get behind the wheel and drive a few blocks home. The streets were mostly empty, and they'd driven home after a few drinks before with no problems, so why would tonight be any different?

While Pirate fumbled with his wallet, trying to extract his ID, one of those drunks briefly fell asleep as he came around the corner. He opened his eyes, realized he was driving, and jerked the wheel as he stepped down on the brakes with both feet. His car skidded hard and careened straight into the back of Rafferty's cab. The impact pushed the cab hard toward the curb, a spot currently occupied by Rafferty's left leg.

There were actually two good things that happened in that moment. One was that Rafferty was standing far enough forward that the tire didn't crush her foot against the curb. Her leg, ankle, and foot were all twisted at an unnatural angle that caused a few bones to fracture in a single quick SNAP, but at least everything was more or less intact.

The other good thing was that the pain and shock were so great that she lost consciousness immediately, and didn't wake up again until an ambulance had arrived with painkillers.

"Herald!"

Hugh, at the card table, looked toward the cashier's cage. "Who is Harold?"

"Not *Harold*," Mick said. "H-E-R... as in her." He pointed toward the maintenance area with the hand not holding the mic. Elise had heard him and was making her way over.

"Your name is Herald?" Hugh said as she passed. "I thought it was Alice."

"It's Elise," she corrected. "What's up, Mick?"

He came closer to the fencing that separated the cashier area from the rest of the garage. Even with his ever-present dark sunglasses, it was clear that he was extremely concerned about something.

"You and Rafferty have become pretty close friends, right?"

"Uh yeah. We've hung out together a few times." Her voice was surprisingly steady. She even managed to keep her smile in place, even though there was a twinge of terror at where he might be going with the question. "She seems like a great lady."

"She is," Mick agreed. "I just wanted to... I didn't want... uh..." He looked at the Reverend, who quickly looked away. "There was an accident."

Elise's smile finally collapsed. "What? Is she okay?"

"Uh," Mick said. "Yeah, I mean, I think so. She will be. It's her leg. Or maybe her foot? The bartender wasn't too sure. He's the one who called 911 and let us know what's going on. He heard someone screaming. Her passenger, apparently. It happened while she was parked, she was out of the cab, apparently a drunk asshole slammed into the parked cab and smashed her leg into the curb. She's on the way to the hospital now. Anyway. Uh. I thought maybe since you were pals, I wanted to let you know."

"Thanks, Mick. I appreciate it. What happened to the cab?"

Mick hooked his thumb at the Reverend. "William is calling a tow truck to bring it back here. You don't have to worry about that, though. You can take the rest of the shift off."

She shook her head. "You don't have to do that."

"Your friend got hurt."

"And if I go home I'll just pace around and be useless. Dealing with a wrecked cab is exactly what I need right now."

Mick looked skeptical, but he nodded. "Let me know if that changes."

Hugh had detected the change in mood and joined them at the cage. "Everything okay?"

"Yeah, everything's fine. Rafferty had a little crunch-up. She's on the way to the hospital to get her leg patched up."

Hugh hissed. "Damn. That's rough." He shifted his weight awkwardly from one foot to the other. "But... uh, since we've confirmed she's okay, can I ask about Cab 521? Is it going to be salvageable?"

"I haven't seen it," Mick said. "When it gets here, I'll let Elise here make the decision."

"No pressure, Harold," Hugh said. "But everyone will hate you if you pull the plug on 521."

She nodded, but she wasn't paying attention to him anymore. The only thing her brain could process was the idea of Rafferty in the hospital. Mick seemed confident the injury wasn't too bad, but did he really know for sure? And what was the scale of badness when it came to a car accident? She drifted away from the cage and headed in the general direction of the maintenance bay. She planned to get her tools ready for the cab's arrival, grateful for the distraction that would keep her from going too crazy.

The cab was in much better shape than Mick and the other drivers had feared. The frame, transmission, and alignment seemed fine, while the majority of the damage seemed to be cosmetic. Just by looking at the impact she could tell that the driver had tried to brake and steer away from the cab before impact. That had prevented him from slamming into the vehicle at full speed, which might also have saved Rafferty from even worse injury.

Mick sent Tim to the hospital to wait for Rafferty and bring her back to the garage as soon as they let her go. Elise immediately dropped what she was doing when he pulled back into the garage near the end of the shift. The rest of the drivers had heard about the accident by that point, and they all made a point to be there when she got back. Elise joined them as they converged on the cab like cattle who had just seen the farmer bringing out the feed.

Rafferty got out of the backseat and leaned against the cab to get her crutches under her. Elise glanced down and saw that her left foot was encased in plaster halfway up the calf, her bare toes sticking out like beans.

"Did they have to surgically reattach the foot?" Doc asked.

"You might be the first cabbie to have an accident when you're not actually in your car," Bob Groom pointed out.

Frank said, "Once you've been driving for a while, you learn little tricks like getting out of the way before the one-ton hunk of metal can hit you."

That one actually made Rafferty smile. "I'll keep that in mind, Frank. Thanks." She caught Elise's eye and her smile softened. "Hey."

Elise swallowed the lump in her throat and forced a smile she knew wasn't fooling anyone. "I, uh, checked out 521. It'll be back on the road in no time."

"Well, that makes two of us," Rafferty said, hitching herself toward the cage on her crutches. "Mick. The doctor wants me to take a couple of days off, but I wanted to let you know I'll be back here ready to work again by the weekend."

Mick looked up from his desk. "No. You won't."

Everyone looked at him, but it was Tim who said what they were all thinking. "If she feels up to driving, I think we can trust her."

"It's my left foot, Mick," Rafferty pointed out. "I might have to hobble around here, but once I'm sitting down I'll be good to go."

Mick said, "And what about pain? What if you're halfway across the Brooklyn Bridge and suddenly you get a shock of pain up your leg that makes you hit the person in front of you?"

"I'll take painkillers."

"No impaired drivers in my cabs," Mick said.

Rafferty exhaled sharply and then closed her mouth so sharply that her teeth snapped together. "Come on, Mick. What am I supposed to do?"

"Recover," he said. "When the cast comes off, your spot on the rotation will still be waiting."

Frank, usually the most laidback of the shift, was suddenly angry. "That's, what, six to eight *weeks?* What's she supposed to do for money until then?"

Mick shrugged. "I'm sorry, Raff. I really am. It's policy, and it's for your safety as well as the company's. We can't have you behind the wheel in this condition." Hugh and Doc started to say something at the same time but Mick held up his hands to stop them. "This isn't a discussion! I hate it, too. But, Raff, the odds of you getting into another accident or being stopped by a cop who thinks you're not fit to drive are too high. And what if you get a fare who needs help with luggage or an old lady who needs a hand getting out of the backseat? You're not fit to drive. My hands are tied."

Rafferty grunted and turned away from him. She did her best to storm off, but she was severely hampered by the crutches. She eventually gave up and took a seat at the card table. Tim sat to her left, and Hugh to her right, with the other drivers crowding around her.

Hugh was the youngest of the group and seemed confused by the panic. "I don't understand. Surely the company will cover her recovery time."

"How long have you lived in America, Hugh?" Doc asked.

"I was *born* in America, you ass."

Doc continued. "We're freelancers, not employees, so they don't have to pay us shit when we get hurt. It's easier to get a new body behind the wheel and forget Raff exists."

"But don't you worry, Raff," Tim said. "We take care of our own here. Just like tonight. Right, fellas? Fifteen dollars from every shift~"

"God, no," Rafferty said. "It's bad enough doing it one night. I'm not going to siphon off all of you for two months. I'll figure something out."

Tim said, "You've got savings?"

"Savings?" she said. "You mean *you* have extra money left at the end of every month to put away and never touch?"

He grunted. "Yeah. Right."

She patted his hand. "It'll be okay, guys. Don't worry about me." She looked around at their concerned faces and swatted at them. "Go! It's the end of the shift. I'm sure you all have better places to be than a coworker's pity party. Well. Former coworker."

"Former and future." Tim stood up and bent down to kiss the top of her head. "If you need anything at all, you know where to find me."

"And me," Frank and Doc chimed in at the same time.

The other drivers echoed the promise of support before drifting away. When Rafferty was alone at the table, she leaned forward and put both hands over her face. Elise quietly approached and took the seat Tim had vacated. Rafferty moved one hand to see who had arrived, smiled, then covered her face again.

"Hey," Elise said softly.

Rafferty grunted.

"If you need someone to drive you home, I'd be more than happy to do it. And getting you groceries or run errands. Anything you need."

Rafferty dropped her hands. "Thank you, Elise. I really appreciate that." She put her hand on Elise's. Instead of patting it like she did with Tim, she left it there. "I might take you up on it. Despite my outrage just now, I'm not sure I *can* trust myself behind the wheel. Definitely not for a twelve hour shift. I just have no idea how the hell I'm going to survive two months with no income."

"Well, if the guys are willing to help you out~"

"I can't take their money," Rafferty interrupted. "They're in the same boat I am. They can't afford to pay it, and I would feel awful being in that much debt to all of them. I'd never be able to pay it back. I have *some* savings. It's not like I'm going to starve. But I might have to rethink how much I actually need electricity."

Elise twisted her lips and looked down at their hands. Her mind was working several equations at the same time. When she came to a solution, she looked up at Rafferty again.

"Can I borrow your car tomorrow?"

"Uh." She blinked, confused by the apparent change of subject. "Sure. I'm not going to be using it. What do you need it for?"

Elise shook her head. "There's just an errand I have to run. It's not important." She put her other hand on top of Rafferty's. "We'll get through this whole mess. You and me. And the guys. We'll get you through this."

"Thank you, Elise. It does help to know I'm not in this mess alone."

Elise smiled. "Not as long as I'm around."

She wasn't sure the plan she had in her head would work, but it was Rafferty's best chance at surviving the next few months. And it was something that had to be done anyway. If she could kill two birds with one stone, it would be worth the awkwardness.

It was time for her to go home.

CHAPTER TEN

RAFFERTY DIDN'T speak for the entire ride home. She was still in shock from the accident to process anything at the hospital. She was grateful to Mick for sending Tim to pick her up, and that gratitude was the only thing that kept her from throttling him as he let the other shoe drop. She knew he was right. She knew he was acting out of concern for her as much as anything else. But he was also following orders from the company's owner. He was destroying her ability to work. And she did have savings, but there was no way they would stretch across two months.

And now she was in the passenger seat of her own car, letting Elise drive her home. It was a strange sensation to be driven somewhere, especially in a familiar car. It helped her come to terms with Mick's decision, though, because she had zero memory of getting into the car or the first half of the trip. She'd been too preoccupied with her own thoughts.

She looked over at Elise. "You haven't been saying anything, have you?"

"No. You seemed lost in your thoughts, so."

Rafferty nodded. "Thank you for driving me home."

"And whatever you need over the next two months," Elise reminded her. "Groceries, errands, just say the word and I'll be here for you."

"Thank you," Rafferty said softly. "I don't suppose you need a roommate."

Elise said, "Sure. It's pretty cramped even for one person, but if you need~"

"I was joking." Rafferty actually managed to smile. "But I appreciate that you didn't have to think about it. You asked to borrow the car for the day, right? I didn't imagine that part?"

"No, I did. Do you need~"

"No, go ahead. Where do you have to go?"

Elise narrowed her eyes. "I'd rather not say."

"That's fine. Just bring it back with a full tank of gas."

"Seems like a reasonable request."

She pulled over in front of Rafferty's building. "Do you need help getting upstairs?"

"No." Rafferty opened the door and began maneuvering her crutches out. "I need to figure out how to do it myself sooner or later. Might as well do it now."

"There's nothing wrong with having someone with you just in case."

Rafferty shook her head. "I'll get up or fall on my ass on my own. But thank you." She hesitated, then reached out and took Elise's hand. "For everything. Not just today."

Elise nodded. "You're welcome. I'm just glad I can help out."

Rafferty turned and put her right foot on the curb, using the crutch as leverage to push herself up and out. She refused to acknowledge Elise behind her, watching her, just as she refused to acknowledge the fact anyone on the street might have been watching the spectacle. It was only a little past five, but there was always the potential for witnesses to humiliating displays like this. She managed to get upright, hissing as she bumped her left foot against the car door. She lifted her hand to wave goodbye, then pivoted on her good foot and began lurching toward the building.

She was grateful when she heard Elise start the car and drive away. She didn't want an audience for what was about to happen, especially not someone she was starting to care about. She sighed heavily, looked at the door, and began the ordeal.

Getting into the building was easy enough, once she figured out how to swing the door open and prop her crutch against it so she could hop over the threshold. She continued across the lobby and looked at the stairs. The doctor had told her to put her weight on her hands, not under her arms. He also mentioned leading with her strong leg, so she placed it on the step. He also said 'feet first then crutches,' even though that felt awkward.

She was tired and out of breath by the time she finally reached the top of the stairs. She had to lean against the wall to fumble her keys from her pocket. A neighbor came out, saw her, and asked if she needed a hand.

"No, I'm good, thanks, have a good day," she said, slipping the key into the lock. She slammed the door, twisted the lock, and dropped her crutches. She was able to use the back of a chair to hop across the living room to the couch. She collapsed on the cushions and laid down. She propped her cursed foot up and stared at the cast.

If she had just been standing with both feet on the fucking curb. If she hadn't tried to help the drunken idiots into the back of her cab. Her entire life might unravel because she was literally in the wrong position at the wrong split-second.

Now that she was in her apartment, with her weight off her leg, she had no idea where she would summon the strength to get up again. Let alone cook a meal, go get groceries, any of the things Elise had offered to do for her. She'd never intended to take her up on the offer but now it was looking inevitable. She was going to be hobbled and dependent on others for the next six to eight weeks of her life, a stretch of time which would also eat away at the paltry sum she'd managed to set aside over the years. She was completely and utterly fucked.

Rafferty took a deep breath and let it out as slowly as possible. "Shit."

About an hour into her trip, Elise realized she should have mentioned how far she intended to drive Rafferty's car. It was more than a little rude to borrow someone's car and return it with four hundred miles added to its odometer. She decided it was too late to make amends now and just kept going. If things worked out the way she hoped and prayed, the wear and tear would be worth it.

She followed the Hudson River north, past where it petered out at Albany. Her breathing got shallower the longer she drove, reversing a trip she'd taken earlier that year. She had been panicked during that trip, driving with no clear destination in mind other than "away." Retracing her steps was making her skin prickle. She realized she was sinking into the seat and tried to force herself to sit up straighter. She ignored the way the trees seemed like they were reaching toward her.

By the time she reached Saratoga Lake, she was struggling to breathe normally. Luckily she didn't have to go very far into the town limits before she arrived at her destination. She flexed her fingers on the steering wheel as she passed a pasture framed on three sides by tall stately trees. She'd left Manhattan early enough that there was still a fine mist of morning dew on the emerald grass, and the whole field shimmered like it was leaking through from a more magical dimension.

"Focus, Lisey," she muttered to herself, leaving the pasture behind her. She followed the wooden fence to the wrought-iron gates that blocked the main drive of the ranch. The gates were emblazoned with the silhouette of a horse rearing back on its hind legs. The driveway was flanked by two massive oak trees which provided support for a large arch bearing the name HERALD RANCH.

Elise parked on the street so she wouldn't block the gate. Instead of using the callbox, she crossed the grass and climbed the four rungs of the fence. She'd been doing the same thing her entire life, and doing it now was as easy as walking through a door even with her anxiety turned up to twelve.

She ignored every signal in her head and heart screaming at her to abort, cancel, run away and marched forward. Voices were echoing from near the house, voices she recognized but chose to ignore. They couldn't see her in this field on the opposite side of the driveway because of a tall stand of trees. For that, she was grateful. She kept her eyes forward on the stables in the distance.

Just as she reached the dirt path that led up to the stables, a man appeared leading a horse. She recognized the horse immediately, Sweetknight, and despite everything she wanted to smile and call out to him. But she restrained herself for fear that the man would think the outburst was about him. Things were about to be awkward enough as it was without starting on a misunderstanding.

He sensed her presence and turned, recognized her, and his back went straight. Sweetknight nickered and shifted at the sudden change in his mood, and he focused on the horse long enough to calm him down. He patted the horse's neck and shushed him until the beast was calm again. By that time, Elise had closed the distance between them.

"Lisey," he said.

She nodded, as if confirming her identity. "Hi, Michael."

Sweetknight nickered again in the silence that swelled between them.

"I'm not back," she said, cutting off what she knew would have to be his first question. "I don't want you to get the wrong idea. I don't intend on staying any longer than I have to."

"Okay." He hooked his thumbs in his pockets and looked down at the ground. "And, uh... um... what is it you have to do?"

"Two things, actually." She cleared her throat. "First, I need you to know we're over."

He exhaled sharply, something that might have been a laugh or a gut-punch. His smile looked strained and painful.

"Yes, Lisey, I sort of understood that from the whole disappearing act. Your fiancée vanishes in the middle of the night, you don't really need a note to explain things."

"I left a note."

"Yes, you did. 'I'm sorry. I can't do this to you.' That's pretty much all you needed to say. It really helped me process everything going through my mind that morning. I don't know why you'd need to ever come back after that."

Elise winced and looked away. She had hated leaving the way she did. But she knew that any other strategy would have led to failure. Talking to him, talking to anyone, would have destroyed her resolve. She knew because it had happened before. She couldn't take the risk.

"I needed you to hear me say the words," she said. "We're over."

"Well." He shrugged and slapped his hands against his thighs. "Okay, then. Do we need to get a notary or something to make it official?"

She shook her head. "No," she said in a small voice.

Michael's jaw was shaking. She couldn't tell if it was from anger or trying to hold back tears. He took a few deep breaths before he spoke again.

"You said there were two things."

"Right." She braced herself, knowing this would be just as difficult. She squared her shoulders and just said it. "I need ten thousand dollars."

He laughed. "What?"

"For my share in SweetKnight. I'm selling you my cut."

"That's ridiculous," he said.

"It's what I need," she said.

Michael looked at SweetKnight as if he was conspiring with her. "You know what this horse could earn in his lifetime."

"I don't *have* a lifetime," she said. "And I need the money now."

He looked at her, trying to read her face. "Are you in trouble, Lisey?"

"No," she said.

"You show up here after months without a word... unless you count those four AM phone calls, of course. And yeah. I knew who they were from. I'm not an idiot." He sighed. "But here you are, out of the blue, asking for ten thousand dollars on a horse that could earn you ten times that in a couple of years. And I'm supposed to believe everything is hunky-dory?"

Elise said, "Whether it is or not, it's not your problem. I just need the money, Michael. It *is* a matter of life and death, just not mine."

"Then whose?"

"It doesn't matter. Ten grand could save someone's life. And I know, to you, it's pocket change."

He laughed. "It's not pocket change!"

"Well, fine, okay. But it's a loss you'll barely notice. You'll make the money back by the end of the year, probably. But if I don't get the money, someone is going to be homeless by the end of the year. Her entire life is going to be ruined. I can't let that happen if I have the ability to fix it." She stepped closer to him. "Please, Michael. I wouldn't be asking if I wasn't desperate."

He stared hard at her. "You swear it's not you that's in trouble?"

"Yes, I promise."

He chewed on his lip and looked at SweetKnight. He tapped his foot on the ground. Then, under his breath, he said, "Ah, hell..."

Elise felt hope blossom in her chest.

"You can keep your stake. We've already raced him a few times since you left. We've got some money set aside for you. I don't know how much, but it should be more than ten grand."

"Really?" she said.

"It's your money anyway. Your mama insisted you'd be back 'fore too long so she set it aside. I can go get it for you."

"Without telling anyone I'm here."

"Your mama would *kill* me if she found out you popped up and didn't visit."

She said, "She doesn't have to find out."

"She might be a little curious why I stole your money."

Elise swore under her breath. "Make something up. Please, Michael."

He looked at her, then turned and scanned the field until he saw a ranch hand. He called him over to take SweetKnight, then walked past Elise toward the house.

"Come on. I'll write you a check."

"Cash."

"*Cash?* You heard me say more than ten grand, right?"

Elise folded her arms over her chest. "If I take a check, the bank will just tell you where I deposit it. I don't want to be found, Michael. There's cash in the safe. More than enough to cover whatever I'm owed. Give me that and write a check to replace it."

He sighed. "Okay. But you're coming with me." He started walking again.

"I'm not going in there," she said.

He didn't stop or turn back toward her. "Fine. Stay here out in the open, in full view of the house. Someone's bound to look out a window eventually."

Elise looked at the house. Every window seemed suddenly threatening, reflecting the sun so that she couldn't see anything within. She swore under her breath and hurried to catch up with Michael.

They entered through the front door. She checked her watch and assumed the rest of the family was either still upstairs or in the kitchen getting breakfast. Michael passed through the parlor, sliding open the door that led to their mother's office. Elise followed like a thief, ducking to one side as soon as she was in so she couldn't be seen from the hall.

The safe was concealed behind a painting of a horse, the first horse the family had owned. Michael swung the painting out and moved closer to enter the code. She had expected a stronger reaction to seeing him, to being in his presence again. She had been terrified that she would forget about Manhattan, Achilles, Rafferty, and just transform back into her old self. But she felt nothing. She just wanted to get her money and get out as quickly as possible.

It *was* terrible being in the house again. It felt stifling, like she'd stepped into a vacuum-sealed museum piece. She kept glancing at the door as if she was afraid it would vanish if she didn't keep it in her periphery. It was a trap. A snare designed to keep her inside.

Michael had the safe open and was consulting a file. "According to this," he said, "we owe you fourteen thousand two hundred eighty one dollars. I think that's all here."

"Round down if you have to," she said. "I don't care."

"It's your money," Michael said.

From the hallway, a woman called, "Michael? Was that you?"

Elise's blood went cold. She backed up until her shoulders hit the wall, wishing there was a plant or a curtain she could duck behind. She went as still as possible and held her breath as Ruth Herald stepped into the office. She walked all the way to the desk, her eyes on Michael, so she completely bypassed Elise without seeing her.

"I thought I heard you come in," Ruth said. "There's a... car parked by the gate. Raymond was hoping you could go and check it out." She finally registered he had the safe open and was holding a stack of cash. "What are you doing?"

Michael looked down at the money. "Ah, Mrs. Herald... This isn't, um..." He looked past Ruth and raised his eyebrows. "You can see how this would have been awkward, I hope."

Ruth turned to see who he was talking to. Her eyes widened when she realized who was cringing in the corner.

"Lisey," she said softly, one hand rising to her mouth in shock. "Oh my goodness. You're back."

"I'm *here*," Elise said. "I'm not back. I just came back to..."

"To get the money she's owed," Michael said.

Ruth looked at Michael, then the money. "You said you weren't in contact with her."

"I wasn't. I haven't been. I'm as shocked as you are that she's here right now."

Elise said, "He's right. This is the first time I've spoken to him since I left."

"And *where* have you *been*?" Ruth snapped. "We've been worried sick about you."

"It doesn't matter," Elise said.

"It doesn't matter?" Ruth echoed. "You vanish without a trace, then you show up all these months later looking like you've been up all night, asking for thousands of dollars? I think we have a right to know you're not caught up in, in some kind of *cult* or something."

Elise almost laughed. "A cult? No. I'm not in a cult, Mom. I just had to leave."

"We're your family," Ruth said. "We care about you, Lisey. If you want that money, you're going to have to answer some questions."

Michael said, "No, she doesn't."

Ruth and Elise both looked at her. "Pardon?" Ruth said.

"She doesn't have to be interrogated." He held up the cash, then put it in a bag. "It's her money. You put it in the safe for her, put it in the ledger. She doesn't have to jump through any hoops to earn it. But before I hand it over, there is one thing I want to know. One truthful answer, Lisey."

Elise said, "I won't tell you anything that will help you track down where I went."

"That's fair," he said. "The question is... are you really okay?"

Her eyes burned. "Yes. I'm okay. I'm happy. There's... I have people who care about me. And one of them is in a lot of trouble, and I want to help. That money can change someone's life."

Michael stepped around the desk and handed it to Elise. "Better than gathering dust in a wall."

"Thank you," she said quietly.

"I didn't do anything." He moved toward the door, then turned to face her again. "And the other thing. The one you mentioned outside."

Elise nodded that she understood.

"It's official. Whatever you need from me, acknowledgement or... whatever... you have it."

"Thank you, Michael."

"I didn't do anything worth thanking me for. Just be safe. And you'll always have a home here." He looked at Ruth and raised his eyebrows. "Right?"

Ruth crossed her arms over her chest and turned away from her.

Michael rolled his eyes. "She'll be outvoted. Take care of yourself, Lisey."

"Thank you," she said.

She stepped around him and left the office. Ruth pursued.

"So that's it? You're just going to leave again, vanish without even a hint about where you're going?"

Elise put her hand on the doorknob. The last time she'd been standing in this position, she really didn't have any idea where she was going or what would happen when she got there. She had some cash in her wallet and a checkbook to withdraw more before she left Saratoga Springs, but she'd had no plan. There had literally been nothing waiting for her on the other side of the door. And yet she'd still somehow found the strength to open it and step through.

"I'm going home." She opened the door and left the house. "I'm going back to Zero City."

CHAPTER ELEVEN

THE KNOCKING woke Rafferty up. It took her a moment to realize she was on the couch, and for the strange weight on her left foot to make sense. She grunted, ran a hand over her face, and considered ignoring whoever was knocking on her door at the ungodly hour of... She checked her watch and saw that it was one in the afternoon. She grunted again. She had planned to wallow on the couch listening to depressing music, but she hadn't even found the energy to go to the stereo before passing out.

There was another knock, louder this time, and she forced herself into a sitting position. Before she could say anything, the knocker announced herself.

"Raff? It's me."

"Elise?" She started to stand, decided against it. "It's unlocked."

The doorknob rattled. "Um. I don't think it is."

Rafferty looked and saw the lock on the knob was upright. She sighed and slumped her shoulders. "Okay, just a second."

She used one of her crutches to stand, then hopped to the door. She unlocked it and stepped back to let Elise inside.

"Shouldn't you be asleep right now?"

"Gosh, that would be great," Elise said. "I hope I didn't wake you up."

Rafferty closed the door and gestured at the armchair. "Doesn't really matter. I've got nowhere to be tonight, so."

Elise sat down and waited for Rafferty to get back on the couch. The mechanic looked nervous, but in a twitchy way. She was holding a leather zip-up bag in her lap.

"There's something I have to ask you. And it's going to sound like it's none of my business, too personal, all that, but just trust me."

"Okay."

"On a good night, how much do you make driving a cab?"

Rafferty considered the question. "With tips? A night where I went home with a hundred fifty would probably be a good night."

Elise nodded, clearly doing the math in her head. "Okay, so that's close to a thousand a week?"

"If I have a week of good nights," Rafferty said, "which has never happened."

"We're talking averages. So, a thousand a week, that's eight thousand dollars you won't get because of this injury."

Rafferty forced a strained smile. "Did you come over just to illustrate how screwed I am? Because trust me, I know."

Elise shook her head. "No, not at all. I'm just working out the math. So eight thousand is the best case scenario. And if you do have to wait eight weeks, that includes Christmas and New Years. Those nights are probably really busy and filled with good tippers."

Rafferty held up a hand. "I'm serious, Elise, what are you doing here? I'm already spiraling."

"Sorry. I just wanted to be sure it was enough."

Elise unzipped the bag in her lap and scooted to the edge of her chair. She took out a stack of money that was about as thick as a paperback book and placed it on the coffee table. Rafferty stared at it. The top bill was a hundred, and the stack was so thick that she suddenly felt strangely cold. She looked up at Elise, who was staring back at her.

"What's that?"

"Ten thousand dollars."

Rafferty kept very still. "What?"

"I was doing the math in the car, and it *seemed* right. And I think without worrying about leasing the cab every night, paying Mick and the Reverend their cuts, paying for gas... oh, I filled up the car for you, like you asked. Uh. Yeah. I think this covers you for the, um, duration of your recovery."

"What?" Rafferty said again.

"You know, what we just talked about," Elise said. "A thousand a week, and if you end up being out for the whole eight weeks, then~"

"What the hell?" Rafferty interrupted. "Why is there ten grand on my table?"

"It's yours."

"Where did it come from?"

Elise shook her head. "That doesn't matter."

"The fuck it doesn't," Rafferty said. "I don't know where you got this cash, but I'm not taking this kind of money from *anyone*. My god. You heard me at the garage. I wouldn't take fifteen dollars a night from the guys. What on earth makes you think this would be okay?"

Elise looked like she was on the verge of tears. "But you need it."

Rafferty grabbed the money and threw it at Elise. It hit her in the chest. "I don't need charity."

"It's not charity!" Elise said. "Look, it's my money. It's money that I didn't know I had before this morning, and before I asked for it, it was literally gathering dust in a wall. There was actually fourteen thousand dollars in the whole thing, but I thought that amount was unnecessary. *That* would have been charity. This is just what you *need* to keep your home, to feed yourself, to get through what you're going through intact. Plus a little extra to cover new expenses like delivery and paying someone to do errands for you or whatever."

She put the money on the table again.

"Please. Take it."

Rafferty stared at the money, then forced herself to look away. "Where did it come from?"

"For God's sake." Elise leaned forward and put her hands over her face. "Can't get the money without saying where it's going. Can't give it away without explaining where it came from. Can I please just have a wall between my old life and what I'm trying to make here?"

"It's ten thousand dollars, Elise."

"I know."

"It's life-changing money."

"It's life-*saving* money, the way I see it."

Rafferty suddenly realized she was about to cry. "I can never pay you back."

Elise said, "I already said it's money I didn't know I had before this morning. And I have more that I'm keeping for myself, so I'm coming out ahead anyway. It's just money, Rafferty. And not having it was about to cost you everything. That seemed so wrong to me. I figured if there was a way I could change things or make them better, I would do it."

"So you're just giving me ten thousand dollars."

"Yeah."

Rafferty reached out and picked up the money. This time she let herself acknowledge the weight of it. She thumbed through it, seeing all the 100s flip by. It all looked real. It was the answer to all her problems. She could already feel the weight and stress evaporating from her shoulders.

"Thank you, Elise."

"You're welcome." She stood up. "I'll let you get back to sleep..."

"Wait, wait."

Rafferty put the money down and stood up. She stayed hunched over so she could use the couch and coffee table for balance instead of getting her crutch. Elise moved closer and offer an arm. Rafferty muttered a thank-you and wrapped her arms around Elise for an awkward hug. She was balanced on her right foot, but she still ended up leaning a lot of her weight against Elise, who didn't seem to mind. Elise returned the hug, squeezing her tightly.

"Thank you," Rafferty said again.

"You're welcome."

The hug continued past the natural ending point, but Rafferty didn't want to let go. Elise actually shifted her hands to make the hug tighter. Her chin was on Rafferty's shoulder, her ponytail brushing Rafferty's face in a way she very much didn't mind.

"I ended the thing."

Elise's voice was quiet, and further muffled by having her lips pressed against Rafferty's shoulder, so she assumed she'd misheard. She leaned back so they were facing each other but without breaking the embrace.

"Sorry?"

"The... thing. That I..." She closed her eyes, and tears appeared on the lashes. "Shit. I was engaged when I left. That's the thing... from before, when we almost..." She sniffled and nodded toward the hallway. "When I got the money, I also made sure that was over."

Rafferty said, "Oh. Okay. You don't have to tell me anything else. You're right, you deserve to choose where your lines are drawn."

Elise looked at her for a long time. Then she said, "Sit down."

Rafferty kept hold of Elise's arm and lowered herself back onto the couch. Elise sat down next to her, both of them facing the same way.

"His name was Michael. He works for my family. We'd known each other forever. Since we were teenagers. We never really dated back then. But when I was around... I don't know... twenty, twenty-five, I started to think it was strange that I'd never really found anyone I cared about. I liked Michael well enough, so it seemed like the right thing to do. I figured maybe movies and books just exaggerated love like they exaggerate everything else. I thought maybe it was enough to be with a nice guy that I liked, and that was what marriage really was.

"We dated for about five years... and we've been engaged for almost a decade. He never pushed me to set a date. I could tell he wanted it to happen but I didn't see any reason to rush. Then I learned about Evelyn Wade, and I thought, 'oh. That's an option?' You might think I'm incredibly naïve but I'd never considered the idea that those... that kind of..." She gestured with her hands. "My family was very religious. Gays were just promiscuous young people in the city. They weren't... they didn't have relationships. They didn't just live their lives like everyone else."

Rafferty said, "You're not naïve. A lot of people think that way, unfortunately."

"Mm." Elise looked down at her hands. "I tried to stick it out with Michael. I wanted to make it work. I told myself I was just curious. But eventually it was all I could think about. I realized that I was settling into being someone I felt like I *had* to be. Faithful wife. Eventually a mother, maybe. Michael and I never talked about kids. And at my age, it needed to be a discussion sooner or later. But it just happened one night. I was laying in bed next to Michael and I realized that I did not want whatever the next day looked like. Breakfast and chores and running errands, repeat forever. With Michael."

"You had to see who you were outside of the bubble."

Elise nodded. "Zero City."

Rafferty chuckled. "You're right. It definitely works."

"It really does." Elise laughed and leaned back, slumping on the couch. "I didn't expect to meet someone like you so quickly. I didn't expect to have feelings for you."

Rafferty leaned back next to her. "It couldn't have been easy to walk away like that."

"God. No." She shook her head and stared at a spot on the ceiling. "There have been times I wished he was cruel. Even abusive. How terrible is that? But he was... he *is* a great guy. I showed up after all this time and his only question was asking if I was okay."

"What a jerk."

Elise laughed. "Right? The least he could've done is act like I was his property."

Rafferty held her hand out. Elise stared at it, then placed her hand on top of it. They linked fingers.

"I'll never forget this, Elise. You literally saved my life with that money."

"Well. I can't think of anything else I'd rather spend it on." She finally turned to look at Rafferty. "I just want to protect you."

Rafferty had no idea what to say to something like that, so she looked away. She felt like she could breathe for the first time since waking up in the ambulance. She barely even remembered being in the hospital, or the drive back to the garage. The entire morning had been a complete blur of panic and her brain trying to shut itself down to avoid thinking about the hole she was about to slide down. She looked at the money on the table. It was such a ridiculously small stack, and it had just saved her.

"I really want–"

She stopped herself when she looked at Elise and saw that she was fast asleep. If she worked an entire shift and then apparently spent most of the day behind the wheel, it would make sense that she would crash the second she completed her mission. Rafferty looked down at their hands, still linked, and decided it wasn't worth the risk of waking her to let go. She rested her head on the back of the couch and stared up at the ceiling.

She was actually pretty tired, too. She'd been dozing off and on, but it hadn't been a restful sleep. She took a deep breath and let it out slowly. Disaster had been averted. She still wasn't entirely sure she was comfortable taking that much money from Elise. But having the offer on the table was enough to make her feel relaxed... and calm... and she knew if she wasn't careful she would drift off...

Elise furrowed her brow. She tried to think of how the sun could be shining on her face from this angle. Or at all, for that matter. She'd bought blackout curtains. Her bedroom should have been completely dark. She cracked an eye and discovered the answer: a window where one shouldn't have been. She opened both eyes and memory flooded back as she saw Rafferty's apartment. She inhaled sharply and sat up straight. Her hand, which was in her lap, pulled something with it.

She looked down as Rafferty withdrew her hand. She was struggling to sit up, eyes squinted shut because she was waking up, too.

"Shit," Elise said. "I'm sorry. I didn't mean to fall asleep..."

"Neither did I." Rafferty rubbed her hand over her face.

"Sorry I woke you up."

"It's fine. What time is it?" She looked at her watch to answer her own question. "Shit, twenty after six."

Elise said, "*Shit.*" She jumped up and banged her shin on the coffee table. "I'm two hours late to work. Mick is going to kill me."

"Oh, shit," Rafferty said. "It's your first time though, right?"

"Yeah, but I doubt he'll be sympathetic to a no-call, no-show who left him hanging for two hours." She scanned the apartment, then patted her pockets. "Can I borrow your car again?"

Rafferty waved her off. "Consider it leased for the time being. I won't be using it."

"Thanks." Elise ran her fingers through her hair. "God, I didn't even change clothes or shower. Damn it."

"Just breathe," Rafferty said. "Go home. Take a shower. Change clothes. Then go to the garage."

"I can't just waltz in three hours late—"

"I'll call Mick and take the blame. I'll explain that I had a really rough day. Depressed and in pain. You were taking care of me. You lost track of time. He'll understand."

Elise sighed. "Are you sure?"

Rafferty picked up the money. "This buys a lot of favors, Elise."

She smiled and let herself calm a little. "Thanks. It's just this is basically my first real job, and I swore I would never do something like oversleep and leave my boss in the lurch."

"A little tip," Rafferty said, "making dumb mistakes like that is part of having a real job. You're going to forget you're on the schedule, you're going to run out of sick days. It's just being human.

Don't worry about it. Mick knows you're reliable on normal days. And he knows this wasn't a normal day."

"Right. Do you want me to come back after my shift?"

Rafferty clearly wanted to say no, but she didn't answer immediately.

"I'll come back," Elise said, saving her from having to ask.

"I don't want to force you into nursing me—"

"I'll come back," Elise said with more force. She softened her tone for what she had to say next. "When I heard you were hurt, I had to stop myself from running to the hospital. I swear, my feet were turning toward the door before I managed to stop them. All I could think about was how I could help. What I could do to ease your struggle. I've never felt that before. Not for anyone. And that was when I realized that my feelings for you went a lot deeper than I wanted to admit. I know the money helps a lot, but I still want to do more. I want to do whatever I can to help you during a difficult time. I want to be here. I want to help you."

Rafferty nodded.

Elise stepped around the table and bent down to kiss the top of Rafferty's head. She didn't know what inspired her to do it, only that it felt right.

"Take it easy tonight, hm? Do what you can, but don't hurt yourself and make things worse. Okay?"

"Okay. Fine."

Elise went to the door, but Rafferty said her name and stopped her.

"You've really never had a real job before?"

She felt her cheeks redden. "No."

"You really are rich, huh?"

Elise twisted her lips, narrowing her eyes as she considered her answer. "My family is rich," she said. "I'm just a mechanic. And I'm late for work. See you in the morning."

Elise's hair was still wet when she ran into the garage. She hadn't bothered to take the time for a full bath, opting to save time by scrubbing up in the sink and pouring a pan of water over her head. It had been a bad idea, but it had at least served the purpose of making her feel less scummy. She stopped at the bank to deposit the rest of the money she'd gotten from Michael, then fought the urge to break a few traffic laws on the way to the garage.

Mick saw her coming and waved her over to the cage. She was

apologizing as she approached. "I'm so sorry, Mick. I completely~"

"Raff called and explained everything. It's okay. We got Matt to cover for you tonight, and you can cover one of his shifts in return. It all works out."

She finally allowed herself to relax. "I'm sorry I let you down."

"It was an unusual day," he said. "You've been golden so far, so I'm willing to let it slide just this once. How's our girl doing?"

"As well as can be expected. She's going to get through it."

Mick nodded. "If anyone can, it's Raff. I feel like shit putting her on the sidelines like this, but if I didn't do it, the owner would just fire me and slot in someone who would."

"I understand. And I think she does, too, or she will when things settle down."

"The bright side for you," he said, "is that Matt's already here. So you can go ahead and take the rest of the shift off."

She started to tell him that wouldn't be necessary, but then decided that she could use the time to continue helping Rafferty.

"I think I'll take you up on that, Mick. If you're sure you don't need me."

He shrugged. "I don't want to imply you're replaceable. But Matty knows his way around the inside of a cab. I think he'll be okay for one night."

Elise started backing away from the cage. "Tomorrow night, I'll be here early."

"Just so long as you show up," he said.

There was a payphone near the drivers' lockers, and she fished a quarter from her pocket. She dialed Rafferty's number and chewed on her thumbnail as she waited for her to answer.

"Hello?"

"Hey, it's me. Uh, Elise. Mick got someone to cover for me, so I thought I'd take him up on the offer for a night off. Is there anything you need from the grocery store?"

Rafferty cleared her throat. "Oh. Uh, yeah, sure. That would be great. Do you have a pencil or something to write a list?"

Elise looked around and grabbed a pencil and a pad off the card table. "All right, I'm ready. What do you need?"

Chapter Twelve

WHEN ELISE arrived with the groceries, she volunteered to put them away and get started cooking something for Rafferty to eat. She paused when she had to name the meal.

"It's nighttime, so I guess it would be dinner," she said. "But you'd normally just be starting your shift, so is it breakfast? I have no idea what kind of food to keep out."

Rafferty smiled and said, "We'll split the difference and call it lunch. You should make something for yourself."

"Yeah?" Elise said. "You wouldn't mind me sticking around?"

"I'd appreciate the company," Rafferty said. "Besides, you've basically been running all over the city for me today. Having a meal with you is the least I can do."

Elise smiled. "Well, thanks. Was there anything on the list you were craving in particular?"

"The tuna melt, if it's not too much trouble."

"I think even I can manage that." She checked one bag and handed it to Rafferty. "Here, you sit a the table and mix everything up while I toast up the bread. Mixing bowl?"

Rafferty pointed to the appropriate cupboard. Elise took down a bowl and handed it to her.

Tuna melts weren't just easy, they had the benefit of being quick. Elise put the finishing touches on the sandwiches, making sure the cheese was nice and bubbly, and plated their dinner. She looked at the dinner table, which was covered with mail, empty cereal boxes, paper towel rolls, and other detritus.

"Um..."

"I normally eat on the couch."

"Ah, okay."

Rafferty pointed at one of the other bags. "And we have chips to go with them...?"

"Absolutely."

She got the chips, added some to both plates. She carried both plates to the living room while Rafferty hopped along behind on her crutches. When she was settled on the couch, Elise put the plate on her lap and sat next to her. The sun had gone down while they were prepping and the living room was mostly dark, but a lamp next to the couch provided enough light that they weren't in shadows. It actually made the room feel romantic, like they were on a date together, but Rafferty knew better than to say that out loud.

"How's your foot?" Elise asked.

"Fine, thanks to painkillers. I'm not looking forward to when they wear off. But for now..." She gave Elise a thumbs up. There was a mild throb in her ankle, and occasionally she moved the leg without thinking and her nerves sent a warning signal about putting weight on it. But the pills definitely were performing miracles at the moment.

"I'm glad," Elise said. "Like I said, I was so... so worried when I heard about what happened. Just a sinking feeling in my gut. I'm really glad the cab was there to work on, or else I would've gone crazy."

Rafferty said, "Oh, how is the cab? Salvageable?"

"Oh, yeah. It got really lucky." She took a bite, realized what she'd said, and put a finger to her lips so she could hastily add, "Sorry."

"No need to apologize," Rafferty said. "I'm glad one of us came out of it relatively unscathed. It makes sense it would've been the one made of metal."

They ate silently for a bit. Rafferty ate a few chips, chewing them thoughtfully as she stared out the window. Finally she decided to say what was on her mind.

"You... you were vulnerable with me earlier. Not just admitting how you felt after the accident. But telling me as much as you did about where you came from. I know you don't like talking about it, or giving details about it. I understand that. I'm sorry I pushed for information."

"It's fine. You had a right to know where the money came from."

"Still, I feel bad. So I thought I'd make things even. I could tell you about where *I* came from. It's not a pretty story."

Elise sat up straighter. "Oh. You don't have to. I would love to know, but if it's something you don't want to talk about it..."

"I want you to know."

They stared at each other across the table. Finally, Elise nodded.

"Okay."

Rafferty cleared her throat, suddenly unsure where to begin. "I told you I grew up in Chicago. My dad was always in and out of jail, so Mom didn't let him come around all that much. Christmas. And for birthdays, if he remembered, which pretty much never did. And Mom liked to hit. She didn't beat me or anything like that. Slaps, mostly. Smacks. Nothing that would ever leave bruises or anything like that. But that probably gives you an idea of why I wanted to get out of there as soon as possible. She hated New York City, so I figured it was the best place to go where I'd never run into her."

"Gosh," Elise said. "I feel like a fraud for implying my parents were terrible."

"Don't," Rafferty said. "It's not a contest. Parents have a million ways to be uniquely terrible, but the end result is always trauma. The only difference is how you deal with it."

Elise said, "The worst my parents did was expect me to be someone I wasn't. Good wife, mother to at least three kids. Basically a carbon copy of my mother for a new generation. They were all about the family legacy. They didn't care if I worked or not, as long as the work I did was related to our business." She paused and then decided to give another detail. "We raise racehorses."

Rafferty couldn't hide her surprise. "Oh. I can't picture you on a ranch."

Elise smiled and raised her glass in a toast. "That may be the nicest thing you've ever said to me. Thank you." She took a drink before she continued. "The pressure got worse when I turned thirty. Getting engaged to Michael took some of the weight off my shoulders, but then I kept refusing to set a date or get pregnant, and they got impatient. I knew that if I hit forty and I wasn't either married or pregnant, they'd do something drastic. I still don't know what form I expected that to take. Like they would force me to walk down the aisle? Drag me to a fertility doctor to make sure everything was okay?" She shrugged and looked out the window. "Anyway. Evelyn Wade. All the questions I needed to answer. And knowing that my family would never give me the time I needed to think. So here I am."

"I'm glad you ended up here," Rafferty said.

"Same. And I'm glad you were here when I showed up. You're the exact person I hoped I would find. So thank you."

Rafferty scoffed and nodded at the table, even though she'd put the money in a safe place as soon as Elise had left earlier.

"I think I should be the grateful one here. You literally saved my ass."

"Well, it's a nice ass."

Elise took a quick drink after saying that, but Rafferty still saw her blush. She laughed, but decided not to tease her about it.

"So after dinner, I'll stick around and help you with the dishes."

"Oh, you don't have to do that."

"I'm more than happy to."

"I can handle it."

Elise raised an eyebrow. "Are you sure?"

"I..."

She looked past Elise into the kitchen. She usually stood at the sink to rinse everything, then loaded everything into the dishwasher. She realized that the dishwasher was to the left of the sink, which would mean she'd have to pivot on her left foot. Elise turned around as well and seemed to follow Rafferty's line of thinking. She faced forward again with a look of victory.

"Smugness is ugly, you know."

Elise grinned. "You'll figure out a work-around in time. But this is the first night. You need to take it easy and save the strategy sessions for later. I know you don't want to admit you need help, but you *do* need help. Anyone would in this situation. I'm here, I took the night off to help, let me help."

"Okay." Rafferty sighed. "I give in. The idea of doing a load of dishes... or god, even going to the laundromat." She rested her elbows on the table and put her face in her hands. "God. I'm going to owe you a lot more than ten thousand dollars by the time this is all over."

"You're not going to owe me anything," Elise insisted. "I'm

happy to help. You just focus on healing and taking care of that ankle."

Rafferty leaned back in her seat. "I'm going to find some way to make this all up to you. I swear."

"Take your time. I don't charge interest."

They finished eating and Elise stood to gather the dishes. She stopped when Rafferty reached for her crutches.

"Where do you think you're going?"

"To the bathroom," Rafferty said. "Don't worry, that *is* something I can do by myself. I managed it a few times already without your help, believe it or not."

"You're practically Wonder Woman."

Rafferty crutched her way to the bathroom, trying not to dwell on how much she would have to rely on Elise, or anyone else, over the next few weeks. She knew that once she got the hang of the stupid crutches she could adjust and get back to some sort of normalcy. But for now, she would have to accept that she needed help with ridiculously easy things like doing the dishes, taking clothes to the laundromat, getting her mail...

She turned on the bathroom light and looked at the bathtub.

"Oh, shit," she muttered. She'd been to the bathroom a few times today already, reveling in the fact it was one thing she could manage on her own. And she'd never realized that she had no idea how she was going to manage bathing.

She looked down at her cast, then back down the hall. She could hear Elise running the water in the sink. Was she humming? Yes, she was humming.

Rafferty looked back at the bath. She usually took showers. But standing was completely impractical, so sitting... with one leg propped up on the side of the tub? She tried to imagine how she would have to twist and maneuver herself to get out afterward. One leg and a lot of slick porcelain... It was a recipe to bust her arm, her hip, or some other bone she couldn't even think of at the moment.

"Shit," she whispered again.

She went into the bathroom and closed the door. She would do what she knew she was capable of, and then she would deal with the horrible, awkward conversation she needed to have with Elise.

There had to be a limit to how far Elise was willing to go.

When she finished in the bathroom, she went back to the kitchen. "I need to take a bath at some point tonight."

Elise turned, eyes wide. "Oh. Right. I guess that makes sense.

What... uh, what... do you...”

“If you could stay, just in case I fall or...”

“Right. Of course.”

“I wasn’t implying you~”

“No, of course not.” Elise laughed nervously. She tucked her hair behind her ears and looked down at the floor. “No. I wouldn’t think so. No.”

Rafferty looked at the ceiling, since Elise had already chosen the floor.

“Trash bag.”

“Yeah.” Rafferty furrowed her brow. “Wait, what?”

“A trash bag. For your cast. You can put it over your cast, and that will keep it from getting wet.”

“Oh yeah. I think the doctor even mentioned something about that. The drawer next to the sink.”

Elise found the bags and peeled one off, handing it over to Rafferty. “I can’t believe part of having a broken foot is that you have to bag up your leg.”

“Maybe it’s not, and we’re doing this all wrong.”

“I wouldn’t be surprised,” Elise said. “But it’s the end result that matters, right? You can go get the bath ready and I’ll finish with the dishes.”

“Sounds like a plan.”

She returned to the bathroom and started running the faucet, then sat on the edge of the tub. She slipped her leg into the trash bag and used an elastic hair tie to keep it up. It felt bizarre, like putting on a loose plastic stocking, and she dreaded the idea of two more months of doing it. She looked back into the tub and remembered seeing scuba divers in movies who would just tip off the side of the boat. She stood up and took off her clothes, sat down again, and hooked her hands on the edge of the tub to slow herself as she scooted backward. She dropped into the water and twisted, keeping her left leg elevated.

Once she was settled, the position wasn’t as awkward as she feared it would be. She could reach the soap and the towel. Things might get dicey when she tried to wash her hair, but she’d figure something out for that.

Elise knocked on the door. “Everything okay in there?”

“Just fine,” Rafferty said.

“I’ll sit out here so you can just call if you need something.”

“Thank you.” Rafferty bit her bottom lip and tried not to feel awkward about talking to Elise while naked. "I really appreciate you helping me today. Not just the money. Although obviously, thank you again for the money. But for everything. I hate to think what it would be like trying to navigate all of this on my own."

Elise said, "It's my pleasure. It feels good to be useful. I spent the morning in a panic, desperate to be with you even though I don't know what I thought I could've done except get in the way."

"Well, now that I know you grew up around horses, I'm glad you didn't show up. I know what you people do with a broken leg."

Elise laughed. "Oh. That's bleak."

Rafferty smiled. "Sorry. I'm in a bleak kind of mood."

"That's probably to be expected."

"Yeah," Rafferty said. "But it's so much better than it could've been. I've probably said thank you a hundred times tonight, but it still doesn't feel like enough."

"I'll let you know if I get sick of hearing it."

Rafferty took a deep breath and closed her eyes. "I hate feeling this vulnerable with someone," she finally said. "I hate relying on anyone else. When you offered to get my groceries, it should have made my skin crawl. If Tim or Mick had offered, I'd have screamed their faces off. With you, though, I just feel grateful."

Elise said, "Part of the reason I never set a date to marry Michael is because I dreaded the idea of being a wife. Buying the groceries. Washing the dishes. I didn't want to be anyone's servant. But I'm more than happy to do it with you."

"Well, this is different because you know it has an end date."

"No," Elise said quickly, but quietly. "That's not why it's different."

Rafferty closed her eyes. "No," she agreed, just as quietly. "I know."

Elise went quiet after that, and Rafferty finished washing up. She was self-conscious about the whole process, knowing someone was just on the other side of the door listening in. It wasn't a bad feeling, and she didn't necessarily hate it. But at the same time it made her less inclined to linger.

When she was done, she practiced standing but discovered she couldn't quite get the angle right. There was a towel hanging within reach, so she pulled the plug with her toe and grabbed the towel. As the water drained around her, she draped the towel over her chest and tucked it under her arms.

"Elise? I need a hand."

"Okay…"

A second later the door opened and Elise stepped in. Rafferty glanced up, then did a double-take and laughed when she realized what she was seeing. Elise had taken Rafferty's denim baseball cap, the one with a small picture of a pizza slice above the bill, off the closet door hooks. She had put it on so that the brim angled down over her face and blocked her view, but she could still see the floor so she wouldn't trip over or walk into anything.

"It's okay," Rafferty said, "I'm covered up with a towel. Though I do appreciate the effort."

Elise pulled the cap up but left it on her head in a more natural position. Rafferty noticed she glanced down at her bare legs for longer than was strictly necessary, but she decided not to mention it. The poor woman was already embarrassed enough judging by the color in her cheeks. She moved closer to the bath and cleared her throat.

"Okay, um. How do you want to do this…?"

Rafferty said, "I think if you just hold my hands, I can get my right foot under me and I can just go from there."

Elise nodded and held out her hands. Rafferty kept her arms tucked so the towel wouldn't fall. She got her foot planted and pushed down at the same time Elise gently pulled her up. Rafferty was suddenly standing, the towel draped over her front but her backside completely exposed. She dropped one hand to Elise's waist and leaned against her, bringing their faces much closer together than she expected. Elise blinked hard a few times, glanced down, then overcorrected and looked toward the window.

"You, um, you can lean on me to step out of the tub…"

"I'm not too heavy?"

"You're fine. I've got you."

Rafferty put her weight against Elise and lifted her foot. Elise held on tight and turned her, fumbling slightly, and instinctively put one hand in the small of Rafferty's back to steady her. Rafferty's back was currently naked, and wet, and Elise inhaled sharply as she pulled it away.

"It's okay," Rafferty said.

"I know." Elise laughed nervously. She glanced down again, but this time her eyes lingered. Rafferty looked down as well and saw their position, combined with the towel and the leftover wetness from the bath, had conspired to give her an impressive décolletage. She looked up and met Elise's gaze. They stared at each other, Rafferty's left leg awkwardly hovering in the air. Elise wet her lips and looked at Rafferty's mouth.

Rafferty leaned in.

Elise pulled back. "No... stop."

Rafferty retreated. "Okay."

"It's not that I don't want to," she said quietly. "But it's like... last time. When you stopped it because it wouldn't have been right. I don't think now would be right, either. You've had an incredibly stressful day. It's only been *one day*, Raff. And your emotions have been twisted up and down and back and forth since the moment you got hurt. On top of all that, you're on painkillers right now. So even if you could make a rational decision about kissing me right now, you might not remember. You might not remember *any* of this, and I d~ That wouldn't be fair to you."

"I really wish that didn't make sense," Rafferty said.

Elise smiled sadly. "How do you think *I* feel? I'm standing here holding a beautiful woman who is naked, wet, and wants to kiss me, and I'm saying no? Are you *sure* it makes sense, because I'm willing to follow your lead on this one."

Rafferty chuckled. She leaned in and pecked Elise on the cheek, then moved her lips closer to her ear so she could whisper.

"When our time comes," she said, "it will be worth the wait."

Elise smiled. "I know. And now we're even. You stopped one kiss, and I stopped one."

"Third time lucky."

"Hope so." Elise stepped back. "Are you good on your own?"

"Yeah." She reached out and braced one hand on the sink. "I'll dry off and put some clothes on."

Elise nodded. "I'll be out in the hall if you need me."

"Thanks." Elise started for the door, but Rafferty said, "Oh and you can keep the hat. You look cute in it."

Elise touched the brim and closed the bathroom door behind her.

Rafferty took a deep breath and blew it out sharply. "Stupid painkillers..."

CHAPTER THIRTEEN

"THERE YOU are!"

Elise was startled by the volume and irritation in Tim Kuberski's voice. She had just arrived at the garage, the door still open behind her, and he was already out of his seat and walking toward her. She knew Tim and Rafferty were close, so she'd always felt like he was also her friend by default. But now, walking away from his card game, she tried to remember if they'd ever had any bad interactions in the time she'd been working there.

"Is something wrong?" she asked.

"Yeah, something's wrong!" Tim detoured to the cage, snapping his fingers. "Mick, gimme the keys to Cab 701, will ya?"

Mick said, "Your shift doesn't start for twenty minutes, Tim."

"I'm not starting my shift. I'm just going around the block. I need this mechanic to hear what's going on under the hood."

Bob Groom said, "I had 701 last night, I didn't hear a peep."

"Yeah, but you've got the ears of a..." Tim tried to think of an analogy. "I don't know, something that can't hear a peep. I just want *her* to hear it so she can *fix* it."

Mick handed over the keys. Tim waved for Elise to follow him. She looked at the other drivers, at Mick and the Reverend, then followed.

It had been strange coming to work the first few days after

Rafferty's accident. She'd gotten used to seeing Raff, to having someone she considered a partner against all the men. Being there without her was like being thrown to the wolves. But it had been okay so far. She'd joined in their joking from time to time, and she'd even gone with them to get a drink after shift once or twice. She didn't think they would ever consider her 'one of them,' but she seemed pretty confident she wasn't going to be treated as an outsider anymore.

She got into the passenger seat of Cab 701. Tim started the engine and strained to hear anything amiss. Most of the cabs had some issue or another. A clack or rattle here or there. The fleet was pretty old and repairs were mostly on an 'as-needed-to-prevent-death' basis. But she didn't hear anything that might have caused Tim's outburst. She leaned forward as far as the seatbelt allowed her, turning her head so her ear was aimed at the dashboard.

"What are you doing?" he asked as he pulled out onto the street.

"I'm trying to hear what you're talking about."

"Oh. There's nothing wrong with the engine."

She looked at him. He sounded completely calm now. Maybe even friendly.

"I just needed to get you out of there so we could talk." He kept his eyes on the road. "Do you know James? Driver on the day shift?"

Elise tried to remember. "I think I met him when I first started. When I tried out both shifts to see which one I liked better."

He nodded. "Probably. Well, over the weekend, it turns out James was caught up in a bust by the boys in blue. He was at a bar. A bar in the West Village." He glanced over. Seeing that she still didn't grasp his meaning, he rolled his eyes. "He was at a *gay bar*, Elise."

"Why did they raid it?"

"Oh, you know, broken windows," he said. "They say they're looking out for the safety of the people who live in the area. Protecting the citizens from, uh, I don't know. Lewd behavior, rowdy drunks, hookers, the 'mentally disturbed.' Whatever sounds the best in the papers. But it was because of what kind of people the bar attracted.

"So. James got dragged downtown. Locked up. Spent Sunday in there, finally had to call the Reverend to come bail him out. And Rev is a good guy, but he's not a vault. He told Mick, who told the rest of us. Frank is pissed. When he first found out, he tried to get James fired. Mick refused but I think only because that would open the company up to a lawsuit. Right before you came in, he was trying to get us all to agree that any cab James uses should be completely sanitized before anyone else has to use it."

Elise said, "God. That's horrible. But wh..." The question died in her throat. "Why are you, um, why do I need to know all of this?"

"I figured you might want to lay low in the maintenance bay when the guys are around, you know? So you don't have to hear that shit. Or they don't ask your opinion on it. Whatever. I just figured you might just want to avoid it entirely."

Elise shook her head. "It doesn't have anything to do with me."

"It..." He looked at her, then back at the road. "It doesn't?"

"Why would you think it did?"

He lifted his hand off the wheel. "Well. You know. You and Rafferty are... you've been... and she told me that she was..."

Elise blushed. "She told you I was like that?"

"No," he said. "She only talked about herself. I just assumed that you and her..." He held up his hand again. "Hey, look, I'm sorry if I jumped without looking. I don't care one way or another about you, or Raff, or Jimmy. Frank is just old-fashioned. And with all that AIDS shit going around, he doesn't want to catch anything, you know?"

Elise's face was burning hotter now. "I'm not like that."

"Okay," Tim said. "My mistake. But the next time you see Rafferty, let her know what's going on down here. Hopefully it will all blow over by the time she gets back."

They had rounded the block and Tim paused for traffic before he pulled into the garage.

"I've never done anything with a woman."

Tim nodded. "Sure. I believe you."

"Never even kissed a woman."

He looked at her. "You know, ah." He cleared his throat. "There's nothing... despite what these assholes might say, you don't have to..."

"I know," she said. "Thanks for warning me about them. I'll be sure to steer clear. It doesn't sound like the most fun conversation."

"Mm."

He pulled back into the garage and parked. When he got out, he lifted his arms in frustration. "Typical! You get a mechanic in the car, and suddenly everything's working perfectly! I should've known."

Elise said, "Let me know if it gives you any more trouble, Tim."

"Will do."

She stuck her hands in her pockets and went to the locker room to change into her overalls. She felt strange. Sick to her stomach, in a way, but not like she wanted to throw up. She hated herself for how defensive she'd gotten in the car. Tim accusing her of being... Not even accusing, just acting on the assumption that she *was*. Why would that offend her? The whole reason she came to Manhattan was because she suspected she was. Her every interaction with Rafferty seemed like it was building to an exploration of it. And God, there had been nights when she imagined how those explorations would go...

But when confronted, faced with the actual words, she'd built a brick wall and ducked down behind it. She was ashamed of herself. She was ashamed to think of how Rafferty might react when she found out. And they'd been doing so well. Elise had been doing errands for Rafferty in her off hours. They'd had dinner a few times, spent a few nights watching TV together. They held hands on the couch during *Night Court*.

They still hadn't kissed. There hadn't been any further bathroom incidents. Rafferty said she'd "figured it out," and Elise still felt too awkward after that first night to press for details. So maybe they were just really good friends. Maybe the attraction she felt to Rafferty was just her emotions being confused by her first real, true friend.

No. That didn't explain the dreams she had. The desires. The ways her brain tried to sabotage her in ways it never had with Michael. She wanted to be with Rafferty, to spend time with her, but she also very much wanted to *be with* Rafferty. Even if she didn't know entirely what that would entail, she wanted to find out. And she wanted Rafferty to be the one who guided her.

Once she was in her overalls, she headed back down to the maintenance bay. She had to pass by the card table on the way, and the guys had resumed their conversation.

"—don't have the resources to assign *anyone* a permanent car," Mick said. "We're not going to block one cab off so only one guy can use it."

"Okay, then just ban him from using *other* cabs," Frank said.

"That's the same damn thing and you know it," Tim argued.

"You're not gonna catch anything from the guy just from driving the same car he drove."

Frank shook his head. "Twelve hours in the car every shift. Sneezing, coughing, doing *God* knows *what* on his breaks. That thing is going to be a petri dish of disease!" He spotted Elise and snapped his fingers at her. "How about a woman's perspective, eh? Hey! Harold! Come help settle something for us."

She wanted to beg off, to claim work, but she drifted over. Tim gave her an apologetic look. "What's going on?" she said.

"It turns out a guy on the day shift is queer," Frank said bluntly. "Mick says they won't fire him, and they expect us to drive the same cabs he does. You think that's right?"

Elise shrugged. "The guy has worked here longer than me. I figure you've driven the same cab as him a couple of times already, and you've been perfectly fine. So I don't know why that would change."

Tim shrugged. "She makes a good point, Frank."

Mick clapped his hands together. "An excellent point! Okay! From now on, I'm not telling *any* of you jokers who had the cab before you. Unless it's an emergency. And Frank, if it makes you feel better, if there are shifts where you have no choice but to drive the same cab James used, you're more than welcome to go home and sit on your ass. Does that deal sound fair to everyone?"

Tim said, "Works for me."

Hugh grumbled his agreement, followed by Bob and Doc.

"Fantastic," Mick said. "Now let's get some of these perfectly safe cabs out on the road, huh? Burke, you're in 430! Bob Groom..."

Elise took the opportunity to slip away from the men, who were now more focused on collecting their keys and trip sheets. When she looked back, she saw Tim watching her. He gave her a thumbs up, and she managed a weak smile in return.

She didn't know if her comment had actually solved anything or just put an end to the argument. But either way she hoped it had earned her enough goodwill to make up for her initial reaction in the car.

Whatever she ended up deciding about herself, she didn't want to be judged for a single knee-jerk reaction to someone thinking she was queer.

Rafferty didn't know how long it took most people to get good at using crutches, but she felt like she'd mastered it in record time. She had no interest in finding out the truth, content to live with her victory even if it was a lie. When there was a knock on her door, she put down the spatula she'd been using, turned on the ball of her right foot, and propelled herself through the apartment almost as quickly as she would've done on two legs.

She opened the door and smiled. "Hey! Did you notice how quickly I answered the door?"

"Tim knows about us?" Elise asked.

Rafferty's smile wavered. "What?"

Elise brushed past her into the apartment. Rafferty checked the hall to make sure no one had overheard. It was a little after four-thirty in the morning, but there was always a chance of eavesdroppers showing up at the exact wrong time. Luckily the hall seemed deserted, so she followed Elise inside and closed the door.

"What are you talking about? Did Tim say something?"

"Oh, Tim had quite a bit to say." She took off her jacket and cap, casually hanging them on the closet door hooks. "One of the day-shift drivers got busted at a gay bar, so it was a topic of conversation for everyone at the garage today."

Rafferty raised her eyebrows. "Wow. I don't suppose they were extremely vocal in their support."

"Tim was, to be fair," Elise said. "The others were talking about sectioning off a cab just for him so they would never have to drive the same one he did. Of course others said it would be easier to fire the poor guy." She pushed her hair out of her face and then let it fall. "Tim warned me to stay away from the socializing areas so I wouldn't get dragged into the conversation. I appreciate him for that. But at the same time, he shouldn't have known to warn me."

"I didn't tell him anything about you."

"Then how did he make the leap?"

Rafferty said, "Because I..." She looked at the floor, suddenly embarrassed. "I told him about *me*, and about a crush I had. I guess he figured out it was you by how I acted around you. Doesn't exactly have to be Sherlock Holmes to connect those dots. I should have told him it was one-sided so he wouldn't make assumptions."

"But it's not..." Elise, clearly angry, suddenly seemed uncertain. "Y-you know it's not one-sided, right?"

"Right."

"Okay. Okay..."

Elise sat on the couch so suddenly that it looked like

something had knocked her down. She slumped forward, elbows on her knees.

Rafferty moved to the couch and sat next to her. "I could have said something so he wouldn't know I was talking about you. I didn't intentionally reveal your secret, but it's still out there because of me. I'm sorry."

The fight seemed to have gone out of Elise. "You don't have to apologize. I'm just..." She sighed deeply and took a seat. "I don't know what I'm doing. Tim grabbed me at the start of my shift, and I've spent the last twelve hours just going over and over it in my head. Wondering if he's told anyone, and what I would say if someone else asked me if I was gay, and I don't know the answer. I told Tim I wasn't. And I felt sick. But it also doesn't feel right to say I *am* because I've never done anything... with..." She looked at Rafferty, then away.

"You don't have to say or be anything," Rafferty said. "If you want to say the past few days have just been friends hanging out, I'd be fine with it."

Elise looked at her, eyebrow arched. "Seriously?"

Rafferty laughed and took Elise's hand. "Yes. Spending time with you is enough. If it leads to something else down the line, great. But I don't need that to make what we have worthwhile. This, right here, is special."

Elise brushed her thumb across Rafferty's fingers. "When did you take your last painkiller?"

"What?" Rafferty furrowed her brow. "Uh, it was a couple of hours ago. I was going to take another one after I had dinn~"

Elise leaned in and kissed her, smothering the end of the word. Rafferty laughed into the kiss, then relaxed and returned it. Elise's lips were pressed tightly together, and Rafferty leaned back just enough to say "Relax," and lightly peck Elise's bottom lip. Elise softened and tried again. The kiss was better this time, still not passionate, but there was no chance of mistaking it for friendly or chaste. It ended twice more, both times continuing after a heartbeat, and each continuation a little more eager, a bit more desperate.

Rafferty pulled back first. Elise followed her but realized the kiss had to end at some point, so she leaned back and turned away. She was smiling like a teenager who had just stolen her first kiss. Rafferty realized that she basically *was* that exact thing, and reached out to touch a loose strand of hair hanging in front of Elise's ear.

"Are you okay?"

Elise looked at her, eyes snapping into focus. "What?"

Rafferty bit the inside of her cheek to keep from laughing. "I asked if you were okay."

"Oh." Elise touched her lips, then looked at Rafferty's mouth. "Uh huh. Yeah." She bit her bottom lip and looked away again. Her cheeks had turned bright red.

She didn't want Elise to think she was laughing at her. She moved her hand to the back of Elise's neck and leaned closer to her. She pressed her lips to Elise's cheek.

"Do you want to join me for dinner? I was making enough food for two, just in case you came over tonight."

Elise nodded. "Yeah. And, um, maybe some TV."

"Sure. I have some *Newhart* on tape."

"Sounds good."

Rafferty nodded. "Okay I should go check on the food."

"I'll help you up..."

"No need. I'm getting pretty good." She demonstrated and smiled down at Elise. "See? I'll be an expert at this by the time I get rid of them. Then I'll have to learn how to walk normal again."

"It's a vicious cycle." She stood up and followed Rafferty into the kitchen. "Can I at least set the table for you?"

"Go nuts. You know where everything is."

She went to the stove and was grateful for the excuse of cooking to turn her back on Elise. The kiss had been amazing, more amazing than she really wanted to admit. She hadn't had a kiss like that in a long time. Maybe ever. She was scared about what it might mean to have a kiss like that, with someone who was comfortable enough in her kitchen to know which cabinet had the good plates.

It was something almost like intimacy, like domesticity, and for the first time in her life, those didn't sound like dirty words.

CHAPTER FOURTEEN

ELISE DIDN'T know if they were going to have sex that night. She thought about it during dinner, keeping her eyes down or turned toward the window to avoid Rafferty's gaze. They talked a little, but Elise couldn't have summarized the conversation afterward. The kiss had been wonderful. The first time she kissed Michael, they'd been young, but that had led to groping and rearranged clothes in the backseat of his car. That had been more enchanting for him than her, but she assumed that was always how it went. Her girlfriends implied guys *always* enjoyed sex way more than women did.

But they were adults now. And, obviously, both were women. Did women do things differently? Because apparently women could give each other a toe-curling, mind-melting kiss and then just go cook dinner. Elise wasn't even entirely sure what they were eating, so she looked down again. Pasta, with chunks of meat and peas.

"Is it all right?" Rafferty asked.

"What?" Elise said, looking up at her. "Oh. The food? Mm-hmm. It's delicious."

Rafferty shrugged. "Just Hamburger Helper. But it's solid."

"It definitely is," Elise said. "I like it every time you make it."

"Next time you go shopping for me, pick out any flavor you like. I'll make it for you."

Elise smiled. "Thanks. That's sweet."

"Sure." Rafferty narrowed her eyes. "Are you sure you're okay? You're being quieter than usual. And that's fine. I just want to make sure you're all right with..." She pointed at the couch with her fork.

"I'm very all right with it," Elise said. "I don't want you to think I regret it or didn't enjoy it. It was absolutely worth waiting for. And if I'm worried about anything, it's that I'll have to wait a long time to do it again. We're-we're fine on the kiss."

Rafferty nodded. "Okay. Are you still worried about the guys at work? I've been there close to a decade, and trust me, this will blow over in absolutely no time at all. They'll forget it and everything will be back to normal."

Elise shook her head. She thought about lying or saying it was nothing. It would avoid an awkward conversation. But she had just spent what felt like a lifetime doing that with Michael, and it had led to her running out in the middle of the night with no intention of ever going back. She refused to let something as stupid as that get between her and Rafferty.

"I'm just trying to figure out if I'm going to... sleep here tonight."

Rafferty sat up a little straighter. "As in... sleep here with me?"

"Yes."

"Oh." Rafferty put her hands on the table, framing her bowl. "Well. Uh. I wouldn't be opposed to that. I'd want to be sure that you're sure that's what you want, of course."

Elise dipped her chin. "Of course."

"And it might depend on if you meant sleep here, or... 'sleep' here. And, again, I'm fine with whatever one you're talking about. If you just want to sleep in my bed with me, o-or sleep on the couch~"

"I was thinking about sex."

Rafferty cleared her throat. "Ah. Okay, then."

"Is that okay?"

"Yes," Rafferty said.

Elise took a deep breath and let it out slowly. "Okay."

"We can finish dinner," Rafferty said. "And then we can watch TV. And we can let things happen naturally. I want you to know I'm okay with whatever happens. All, um, all the options. The ball is in your court here. We can go as far as you want, as fast or slow as you want."

Elise felt the weight lifting off her shoulders. "Thank you, Rafferty."

"You're welcome."

They went back to their meals and, with the hard topic breached, quickly finished eating. Rafferty felt like the room had been cleared of smoke now that they'd addressed the elephant in the room. Now that they'd established Elise would be spending the night - even if the finer points weren't fully established - it was easy to relax and focus on the moment in front of them. When Rafferty pushed her plate away, Elise did the same even though she still had a bit left.

"Full?" Rafferty said.

"Yeah. Not very hungry."

Rafferty nodded. "We can just put it in the fridge. It heats up pretty well."

"Mm-hmm." She twisted to look into the living room, at the TV. "I'm... I'm actually not really in the mood to watch TV."

"That's fine. So."

Elise swallowed hard. "An early night? Or, um, day, I suppose... God, I've never figured out the terminology for going to bed at dawn."

"I usually just say 'night' for sleeping and 'day' for when I'm at work," Rafferty said with a laugh. "Keeps things from being too confusing. And we can call it an early night, if that's what you're sure you want."

"I am."

Rafferty nodded. "Okay. That works for me. I'll go start getting ready for bed."

Elise stood. "I'll clean up in here. I'll, um. I'll be in there in a minute."

"Okay."

Elise took their dishes into the kitchen. Rafferty retrieved her crutches and headed into the bedroom. She turned on the light and scanned the area for any mess, dirty clothes, anything left out that might be embarrassing. She pulled back the blanket to make sure the good sheets were on the bed and the pillowcases were all smoothed out. She'd been slacking on the chore of making the bed each morning, since it had turned into a huge pain in the ass thanks to her leg, but she was grateful she'd taken the time that day.

She considered undressing, but she felt that would be too pushy. Instead, she turned off the overhead light and turned on the lamp next to the bed. It made the bedroom bright enough to see, but it was less harsh and more suited to a romantic atmosphere. If a romantic atmosphere was, indeed, what they needed for tonight.

"Relax, Raff, damn," she whispered to herself.

She sat down on the foot of the bed and placed her crutches on the floor, then pushed them back under the duvet. She didn't want them to be involved with whatever was going to happen tonight. She ran her hands through her hair, shifted nervously, and looked at the bedroom door, which she had left open just a crack.

"Do you want me to turn out these lights?" Elise called from the living room.

"Yes."

She saw the glow from the living room lights go out. Her adrenaline spiked, and she silently scolded herself. She wasn't a teenager waiting for her first girlfriend to show up. She'd done this plenty of times. Elise was the one who should be feeling this frisson of fear and excitement and worry. Her fingers tapped a rapid beat on the blankets. She curled them up against her palm and pinned them with her thumbs to try keeping them still.

The bedroom door opened and Elise stepped inside, then closed it behind her. She leaned against it and looked at Rafferty.

"Hi."

"Hi."

Elise wet her lips. "I was thinking about what would happen when I came in here."

"Yeah? Come up with anything?"

"A couple of things. I'd like to kiss you again."

Rafferty said, "That's... yeah, that works with what I was hoping for, too."

Elise smiled. She stepped forward and bent down. Rafferty leaned toward her and they met halfway. The kiss was firm, insistent, and Rafferty felt the shivers fade with each passing second. She parted her lips and breathed out, sharing the breath with Elise, who responded by slowly sinking down to her knees. Rafferty parted her legs and Elise instinctively moved between them, becoming framed by Rafferty's thighs. She pulled at Rafferty's bottom lip with both of hers, almost like she was tasting her, and Rafferty responded with a quick flick of her tongue.

"You kiss so..." Elise angled her head so that her forehead rested on Rafferty's. "I don't know. It sounds stupid. Your kisses are firm. But so soft. I don't know how you do both, but it feels... it feels real. I'm sorry, that's dumb."

"It's not," Rafferty said. "Come here."

She cupped Elise's cheek and kissed her again. "I'd be okay if this is all we do tonight," she said when they parted again. She brushed her thumb over Elise's bottom lip. "There isn't a point of no return. We only go as far as you're comfortable with."

"I appreciate that." She kissed the pad of Rafferty's thumb, then took it into her mouth. She sucked it gently. "When I kissed Michael, sometimes I would think 'this is fine. I could do this for the rest of my life. It's not that bad.' But when I kiss *you*... it's more like... I *have* to do this for the rest of my life, just to get enough of it." She laughed, a quick and nervous sound. "Sorry. That probably sounds really scary and clingy. I know this isn't, um, any kind of... I know it's just~"

"I understand the sentiment," Rafferty said, smiling. "And it's good that you feel that way. It should feel that way the first time."

Elise nodded. "Yeah." She looked down at Rafferty's body. "I'm not sure where to rest my hands. Can I put them~"

"You can put them wherever you want."

"Okay."

She rested them on Rafferty's hips, then moved higher. She made as little contact as possible as her palms skimmed Rafferty's T-shirt. She paused at her breasts and then, inhaling quickly, rested her hands there. She breathed out and looked up into Rafferty's eyes to make sure she still had consent. Rafferty smiled and nodded slightly, leaning forward into Elise's touch.

Rafferty leaned in and kissed Elise's cheek. "I like that."

"Yeah?"

"Mm-hmm." She slid her arms around Elise's waist. "Is it okay if I touch you, too?"

"Yes. I'd like that."

Rafferty's lips were right next to Elise's ear. "I'd like you to say it."

Elise chuckled nervously. "I want you to touch me. And I want to touch you." Her fingers plucked at the cotton under them. "I want to take this shirt off of you."

"That would be very nice."

They pulled away from each other. Elise moved with a bit more speed now, reaching down to the hem of Rafferty's shirt and pulling up. Rafferty lifted her arms and let the shirt be peeled off of her. Elise tossed it away and reached around her. Elise's fingers were warm as they slid up Rafferty's spine and found the clasp of her bra. She pinched and twisted, then bit her lip.

"I've never done this from this angle," she said.

"It gets easier," Rafferty assured her.

The clasp came loose and Elise gasped. Rafferty shrugged the straps off her shoulders and let Elise take the bra off of her. Elise looked down and her lips twitched into a smile. Her eyebrows were arched, eyes wide and unblinking, and she gently placed her hand on Rafferty's bare left breast. She turned her wrist to take the weight of it, then circled the nipple with her thumb.

"Wow."

"Good wow?"

Elise nodded. Her eyes were shining in the dark. "I looked at magazines. I've *been* looking at magazines. Since before I left Michael. Just to be sure I, that I was actually attracted to... that I wanted..." She wet her lips and finally tore her gaze off Rafferty's chest. "This is better than the magazines."

Rafferty laughed and leaned in to kiss her. Elise moaned softly and squeezed Rafferty's breast.

"Do you want to kiss them?" she asked against Elise's mouth.

"Uh-huh," Elise said. "I want to kiss your breasts, Raff."

"I want that, too."

"Since we met," Elise said, "I've been thinking of all the places I wanted to kiss you. It's been driving me crazy. And now that I'm here, now that we're like this, I don't even know where to start."

"Just start," Rafferty said. "We'll go from there."

Elise bit her bottom lip and gently pushed Rafferty down until she was lying flat on the mattress. Then she got up off the floor and straddled her legs. She put her hand on Rafferty's stomach and smiled down at her, raising her eyebrows.

"Is this okay?"

"Unexpected," Rafferty admitted, "but I don't hate it. Keep going."

Elise nodded. She bent down and pressed her lips to the hollow of Rafferty's throat. Rafferty closed her eyes and brought her hands up. She found the knot of Elise's ponytail. She realized she'd never seen the other woman with her hair down, she began working the elastic to see if she could get it loose without pulling Elise's hair too much.

She managed to get it free just as Elise's mouth closed around her nipple. She gasped and raked her fingers through Elise's hair, freeing it and letting it fall.

"Your nipples are so pink," Elise said, kissing one and then the other. "And freckles! You don't have these freckles anywhere else."

Rafferty smiled down at her, still stroking the waves from her hair. "I had them on my face growing up. They faded, though. I never liked them growing up. Redhead and freckles, bad combo."

Elise looked up at her. "If I'd known a little redheaded freckled girl named Sally, I might not have wasted so much of my life with Michael."

"I think you're getting bold, Miss Herald."

"Wait 'til I get going."

The boastfulness of her statement was somewhat diminished by the shy grin and red cheeks that came with it, but Rafferty wouldn't have had it any other way.

Elise moved lower and kissed Rafferty's stomach. She moved her hand along the waistband of Rafferty's jeans and teased the button.

"Would you..." She licked her lips. "I-I'm not sure what I'm going to be doing here, so if you want to, um, tell me what to do."

"I can do that," Rafferty said. "Unbutton my pants."

Elise did as she was told. Rafferty lifted her hips and Elise hooked her fingers in the beltloops, dragging them down her hips. When she reached the top of the cast, she furrowed her brow but quickly managed to get the denim over it and off. The jeans were tossed aside and Elise faced forward again. Her eyebrows rose, and she gently laid her hands on Rafferty's bare thighs.

"Oh," she said.

Rafferty raised an eyebrow. "Oh?"

"Mm-hmm."

Elise massaged Rafferty's inner thighs with both thumbs. She slid her hands higher. Her breathing had become deep and slow. Rafferty read her hesitation as uncertainty. They were definitely moving fast, and she didn't want Elise to think anything was being asked of her that she wasn't ready for.

"If you want to go back to kissing me, that would be fine."

"Okay," Elise said, then bowed her head and eased Rafferty's legs farther apart.

Rafferty said, "I was actually talking abo~" Her breath caught in her throat and she closed her eyes, turning the word into a gasp. She put her hand on top of Elise's head and fell back to lay on the mattress.

"Okay," she said when she could talk again. "There... kissing there is good, too..."

They lay together in the dark afterward, Elise curled in Rafferty's arms. She was stuck in a loop of the past twenty minutes. No, had it been an hour? Two hours? She had worked up a sweat, and she was still kind of catching her breath, but how much of that was just due to excitement and adrenaline?

However long it had been, her brain kept snapping back to the beginning. To Rafferty's thighs twitching and trembling against her cheeks. To the sound of her moaning and encouraging more, harder, slow now, fast, right there. Elise was sure she hadn't followed every direction, but she'd done her best. And she'd certainly gotten the results they both had hoped for. She ran her tongue over her lips again and smiled. It would be a long time before she forgot that taste.

Her head was on Rafferty's chest. She could smell her sweat and hear her heartbeat. She could feel it as well, a steady thump on her cheek. Every time Rafferty breathed in, Elise's head lifted. When she breathed out, it was a steady breeze across her hair. It was like the gentlest of seas, and the rhythm was about to put her to sleep.

She looked down and saw Rafferty's hand on her hip. Just seeing it made her shudder, and she reached down to touch the fingers. Fingers that had been inside of her just a few minutes earlier, which had done things to her she still wasn't entirely sure she understood. But she wanted to understand. Oh, she was desperate to understand, and revisit, and duplicate what they had been doing.

"Are you okay?" Rafferty asked.

"I'm okay," Elise said. "Did I do anything wrong?"

Rafferty kissed her hair. "Not a single thing. You were amazing."

"I wish I hadn't gone first," Elise admitted. "You did some things that I want to try out."

"We can do it again, if you want."

Elise lifted her head and looked at Rafferty. "We can?"

Rafferty smiled up at her. "Sure. Round two is a lot of fun. Usually slower." She reached up and brushed Elise's hair out of her face. "You look so beautiful with your hair down."

Elise blushed and looked away. She was treated to a view of Rafferty's naked body.

"I think I'm too tired for a second round."

"Oh, good," Rafferty said. "I am, too. But I was willing to push through."

Elise laughed. "Such a martyr, huh?"

"I sacrifice," Rafferty said. "I give and I give."

"Yes, you do."

Elise bent down and kissed Rafferty's lips. She meant for it to be a quick peck, but it morphed into something slow and exploratory. Rafferty's tongue had been inside her, too, working in harmony with her fingers at one point in a marvelous way.

"We'll sleep," Elise said, "and then round two?"

"That sounds perfect." She gestured to the other side of the room. "You can borrow a shirt if you need something to sleep in."

Elise looked toward the dresser, then back at Rafferty. "If...?"

"Yeah. If. I don't know if you sleep naked."

"It depends. I think today, it's the only option."

Rafferty opened her arms. "Then come here."

Elise lay back down and cuddled close to Rafferty's side. She closed her eyes and listened to Rafferty's breath, her heartbeat, and the sound of the city outside the window, letting the combined music carry her to sleep.

CHAPTER FIFTEEN

"HOW CAN you not like X-Men?"

Rafferty shrugged. "It's not that I don't like them. I don't like books about teams. There are too many characters and storylines to keep track of. I like comics that focus on one character. Give me a Kitty Pryde solo series, and I'd be all over it."

Elise smiled and slipped *X-Men* back into the box. "Well, you make an excellent point."

"Thank you. I've given it a lot more thought than I probably should have."

Elise chuckled and continued scanning the covers. They were at Illywhacker Comics, a shop in Hell's Kitchen where Rafferty had a pull list of titles. She'd initially been against going to pick up that month's books, but Elise said she'd never actually been in a real comic book store. They were sold at the gas station near the ranch, and she didn't know if Saratoga Springs even had a whole store dedicated to the medium.

She had no idea there were so many titles, and so many issues for each one. It was daunting. She wondered how anyone ever managed to keep up with any of the stories. Maybe Rafferty had a point about books that only focused on a single character.

They browsed for a while, stopping so Rafferty could explain one character or another, and Elise picked out a few books that seemed interesting. The gas station tended to only get big titles like *Batman* or *Captain America* and she was excited to find some more of the lesser-known stories.

When they left the store, Elise carried the bags so Rafferty's hands would be free for her crutches. She stopped and watched as Rafferty hitched her way along the sidewalk.

"You're already pretty good at that."

"Yeah, I'm a natural. Tell Mick when you get to work tonight. Let him know I can handle myself just as well as ever."

Elise said, "I would do it if I thought he'd cave."

Rafferty sighed. "Yeah. Can't have me behind the wheel on painkillers, but Bob's been drunk on duty a hundred times. And if Mick actually believes Hugh's cab always reeks of pot because of his passengers, then he's an idiot."

"I know," Elise said. "It's unfair. But he does have a point."

"Yeah, yeah." Rafferty muttered. "I just don't do well sitting around doing nothing."

"You aren't 'doing nothing.' You're healing. You're taking the time you need to be sure that--"

Rafferty stopped and held up a hand. "Hold on. Wait." She was smiling now, which Elise found unsettling given the topic of conversation. She pointed up ahead. "Have you ever been in one of *those* stores?"

Elise followed her finger to a glass door set inside a blacked-out stoop. She didn't see any kind of sign announcing the name of the shop, but a silver 6-3-3 stood out among all the black. The windows on either side of the doorway were blocked by posters of women in various states of undress. Signs warned that customers had to be eighteen to enter and IDs were checked. While she was looking, a man in a gray sweatshirt and sagging jeans walked out. He had a baseball cap pulled low over his eyes.

"What is it?" she asked, even though she was positive she knew the answer to that question.

"You said you looked at magazines, right?" Rafferty said. "Where did you get them?"

Elise blushed. She'd gotten them from the bottom drawer of Michael's dresser, but she didn't want to admit that in the middle of the street where anyone could overhear.

"That's a..." She dropped her voice to a whisper. "Porn shop?"

"Yeah." Rafferty grinned. "Let's go in."

Elise's eyes widened. "Let's not!"

"Come on." Rafferty looked around, then started toward the shop. "It'll be fun."

Elise wanted to stop her, but she also didn't want to draw any unnecessary attention to them. She hurried after Rafferty, suddenly irritated at how good she was with the crutches, and caught the door just as it was swinging shut. She stopped just inside the threshold, frozen like a deer in headlights with her shoulders hunched near her ears.

It took her brain a second to catch up with her eyes, for her to process the fact that it looked like a normal video store. The boxes had much different art than the other stores, of course, but it was otherwise unremarkable. Closer inspection revealed the merchandise along the wall to be horrifically lewd, but she felt safe enough to relax her posture and follow Rafferty down one of the aisles.

"What if someone sees us?" she whispered.

"Anyone who sees you is also in here," Rafferty whispered back, scanning the videotapes. "See anything you like? My treat."

Elise pinched Rafferty's sleeve, tugging gently. "No! I don't want anything in here." Elise glanced at one of the boxes and quickly averted her gaze. She didn't think her face could get any hotter. "Can we please just go?"

Rafferty gave in. "Okay."

"Wait. Really?"

"Sure. If you're this uncomfortable, I don't want to be here, either." She touched Elise's hand. "I wanted to push you a little bit, not throw you off a cliff. I thought you might want some inspiration. I didn't think it would be this much."

Elise hesitated. "Well... now I'm not sure." She looked around again. "I've never been in a place like this. I've never... okay, I've never really done *anything*. I'll be forty in a few months and I spent my entire life on that ranch, following a plan someone else came up with. Being in the city, being on my own, being with *you*, it feels like I'm a teenager."

"There's nothing wrong with being nervous," Rafferty said. "And there's nothing wrong with figuring out what you want. That includes sexually. But we don't have to rush it. I won't bring you back here until you're sure you're ready."

"What if I'm never ready?"

Rafferty shrugged. "Then we won't come back. We don't need this stuff. We're doing just fine on our own, right?"

Elise managed to smile at that. "Sure. Yeah. I mean, I think so."

"Me too. So this can wait. Or it can be ignored. Whatever you want." She nodded at the door again. "C'mon. Let's go home."

Elise turned and led the way out of the aisle.

Since that first night, she and Rafferty had spent more time in bed than anywhere else in the apartment. And she couldn't blame Rafferty for most of it. She was the demanding one. She was always asking if they could try a new position, if they could 'lay down for a little while.' She just couldn't get enough. They had sex, they watched each other touch themselves. And it wasn't just the sex part. It wasn't just the way Rafferty's thighs shook just before she came, or the noises she made. It was everything all around that. The soft touches before. The whispered words after. Being physically together was just part of something bigger that she didn't even have the words to describe.

But still, they had fully explored the physical, as far as Elise was concerned. They had done so much and she was so overwhelmed by how it felt that she was a little scared of discovering how much more might be out there. She couldn't even think of different~

Her thoughts stopped dead, and she only realized she had stopped walking when Rafferty bumped into her from behind.

"What's wrong?" Rafferty asked, following Elise's line of sight.

She was looking at a row of boxes at the end of the aisle. The artwork on the outside depicted phallic shapes with thin black belts attached.

"Oh-ho," Rafferty said, chuckling quietly. "Sure. Why waste time on a movie?"

"What? No. I'm not... I-I wasn't..." She shook her head quickly. "Let's just go."

Rafferty hooked her hand around Elise's elbow. "Wait, Elise. We'll go if you want, but first answer one question for me."

Elise looked at her, raised her eyebrows. "Fine."

"Do you really want to go, or do you feel like you *should* go?"

"I want~" She pressed her lips together. She crossed her arms and looked down at her feet. "I don't know."

Rafferty said, "That's a fair answer. So how about this? We leave, go home, and in a couple of days if you decide you want to come back here and take me up on my offer, we'll come back."

Elise raised her eyes, looking at Rafferty through her lashes. "We can go?"

"Of course we can go. Like I said, I wanted to take you out of your comfort zone, not... make you uncomfortable. I know that I just contradicted myself~"

"No, I understand what you mean." The tension faded from her shoulders. "Thank you. I think we should just go home."

Rafferty moved her hand to squeeze Elise's shoulder. "Okay. I'm sorry. I went too far."

"No, you didn't. I just think we should go."

"Then let's get out of here."

Elise said, "But we should buy that first."

Rafferty stopped, looked at Elise, then looked at the strap-on she was pointing to. "Are you sure?"

"Unless it costs, like, a thousand dollars or something..."

"No," Rafferty chuckled. "It doesn't cost a thousand dollars."

Elise crouched to pick up one of the boxes. She looked past Rafferty to the male clerk, who hadn't even looked up from his newspaper the entire time they'd been in the shop. It occurred to her they'd have to interact with him to buy the... item... and she almost backed out again.

"It's okay." Rafferty seemed to read her mind. "He's sold hundreds of them. It doesn't even register to him anymore. Come on."

They walked up to the counter. Rafferty added a bottle of lube to their order, and Elise bit down on a whimper. The man finally put down his paper and rang up their total. Rafferty handed over the cash, accepted her change, and turned so she could put their new toy in the bag from the comic book store.

"Have a nice day, ladies." If there'd been a hint of innuendo or suggestion in his voice, Elise would have exploded in a burst of humiliated smoke. But he just rested his elbows on the counter again and went back to his paper. She glanced over her shoulder to make sure he didn't leer at them as they left, grateful when the door finally closed behind her.

The sidewalk felt like another world. She breathed in deeply, wrinkled her nose at the reek of exhaust fumes, and straightened her coat.

"I don't know how you shop in places like that."

Rafferty laughed. "Well, I'm not exactly on their rewards program. But you've gotta get your smut somewhere. They have a good selection and good prices. And if you'd needed that guy to help you find something~"

"Oh *God*."

"~he would've been very knowledgeable and happy to help."

Elise put her hand to her forehead. "I'm going to throw up."

Rafferty grinned and pointed with one crutch. "Go. We're going to miss our train."

They used the toy the next night, when Elise got home from work.

Elise found it much easier to have the discussion in the privacy of Rafferty's home. They ate dinner and worked out the specifics. Rafferty would be the one to wear it, which she was fine with. She confessed that she wasn't a very big fan of penetration with anything thicker than two fingers. Elise hadn't considered that. She'd looked over at the table where the box was waiting in the comic store bag like a loaded gun.

"What does it mean that I want it?"

"How do you mean?" Rafferty asked.

Elise said, "Penetration. What does it mean that I'm... asking you to put on a... to wear a..." She looked over at the bag again. She still didn't want to say the specific words. "To wear *that*."

Rafferty understood anyway and put down her fork. "It means that's what you like. Or what you're exploring to find out if you like. That?" She pointed at the bag. "Doesn't get to decide who you are. That's just a means to an end. You had *that* built in with someone, but it wasn't enough. And if you want to add *that* to what we have, it doesn't mean you're unsatisfied with me. It just means you want something different. Your sexuality isn't about how you fuck. It's about how you feel. Everything else is just... I don't know. Kink."

Elise laughed.

"You might be gay. You might be bisexual. In the end, it doesn't matter as long as you're happy with the person you're getting in bed with."

"I'm definitely confident on that much, at least," Elise said.

Rafferty smiled and picked her fork up again. "Finish your food."

They finished eating, did the dishes, and then went into the bedroom. Rafferty suggested washing the toy in the bathroom sink before doing anything with it. She offered to take care of the task and told Elise to undress and wait in bed. In the bathroom she took off her own clothes and hung off her crutches as she washed the toy. The soap and water made it feel too lifelike in her hands, which was awkward for the situation but hopefully would enhance the experience for Elise.

Once it was ready, she took it back into the bedroom. Elise was sitting on what Rafferty already thought of as "her" side of the bed. She had her back to the headboard, her knees up with her arms wrapped around them. She'd undressed down to her panties and her undershirt, but it was clear she'd taken off the bra underneath. Elise's eyes went noticeably wider and she sat up straighter.

"I hope I don't get used to the sight of you naked," she said.

Rafferty held her hands out to either side and cocked her hips, then moved the toy so that it was in front of her crotch. "What do you think? Does it look weird?"

Elise's tongue touched the corner of her mouth. She shook her head. "No. Not weird at all."

"If there's a point where you want to just go back to the normal way, just say the word."

Elise nodded and scooted to the edge of the mattress. "Do you want me to put it on you?"

"I was hoping."

"Come here."

Rafferty moved closer. They figured out the harness and got it settled on Rafferty's hips in a way that felt comfortable. Once it was in place, Elise took the toy in her hand, lifted it, and pressed a kiss to the shaft. Rafferty breathed in sharply, eyebrows rising at the reaction she had to the sight. She couldn't feel the kisses, but she could see Elise's lips parting, could see her tongue running along its length, and her brain connected the dots in a way that she found very, very surprising.

Her annoyance at the crutches hit a high peak. She wanted nothing more than to plant her feet and put both her hands in Elise's hair and just...

She grunted and rolled her head back. "I can't believe what this is doing to me."

Elise laughed. "Nice?"

"It's... very appealing. Yeah." She looked down and took one hand off the crutch, brushing Elise's bangs away from her face. "Is it what you hoped?"

"It's more."

Then, keeping eye contact, Elise angled the toy upward and took it into her mouth.

Rafferty moaned and arched her eyebrows, straining not to

break eye contact. Her hips moved of their own accord, thrusting gently, pushing more of the toy into Elise's mouth. When she gagged, Rafferty whispered an apology and they found a slower rhythm. She let Elise go on as long as she could bear with her weight on one leg, then gently pulled away from her.

"I need to lay down, sweetie."

"Oh. Here, swap places with me."

Elise stood, and Rafferty gratefully lowered herself down onto the mattress. Once Elise was standing, she peeled her T-shirt off and hooked her hands in the waistband of her underwear. She bent at the waist to take them off, shaking her foot to get them out of her way. She straddled Rafferty, both hands on Rafferty's shoulders for support, and planted her knees in the mattress on either side of her waist. Rafferty used one hand to support Elise, fingers splayed in the small of her back, and reached between them with her other hand.

"Are you ready?"

Elise nodded, leaning back as far as she dared. Rafferty kissed Elise's chest, then rested her cheek against it as she guided the tip of the toy where she needed it to be. Elise gasped, then inhaled sharply, and then slowly sighed. She took one hand off Rafferty's shoulder and put it between her legs, both of them working to line their bodies up right.

Rafferty furrowed her brow. It was harder for her because she couldn't actually feel what she was moving around, but she thought she was almost—

"Oh-ohhh..."

Elise collapsed forward against her and sank down. Her thighs tightened around Rafferty's waist. She arched her back and pressed her face to Rafferty's throat. She opened her mouth and lazily licked a heart on the warm skin.

"You're inside me," she whispered.

"I know," Rafferty said. She kissed Elise's shoulder and pressed her hand into Elise's back, urging her closer. "We can stay like this as long as you want."

Elise shivered, then nodded. And then, a moment later, she pulled her hips back and sank down again. Rafferty hissed through her teeth.

"Good or bad?" Elise asked.

"Good, good," Rafferty said. "Keep going."

Elise said, "Okay," and rolled her hips, causing Rafferty to moan again. "H-how long is it s-supposed to take?"

Rafferty shook her head. "Doesn't matter. Quick is fine."

"Good," Elise shuddered again. "Okay, good. That's..." She lost her words and began to breathe heavily against Rafferty's neck. "Thank you, Rafferty."

"Come for me, Elise."

Elise moved faster, breathing harder, and shifted backward. Her face was flush and beaded with sweat, and she was grinding hard on the toy. Rafferty locked eyes with her and nodded, and Elise bared her teeth. She grunted something that might have been "oh shit," and then her entire body clenched like a fist. She curled in on herself, her legs squeezing Rafferty in a vice, her chin against her chest, and a wave passed through her from head to toe.

When it was over, she breathed out with an explosive grunt. Her body went limp, and she collapsed forward against Rafferty.

"Oh my god," she whispered. "What was that?"

"I think it was an orgasm," Rafferty said. "Are you okay?"

Elise nodded. "I think so."

Rafferty reached between them to slip the toy out. When her fingers brushed Elise's folds, Elise jerked away from her with a squeal.

"It's okay," Rafferty laughed. "I'll go slow."

"Just-just wait a second..."

"Okay." Rafferty guided Elise's head to her shoulder and stroked her hair. "We can wait as long as you need, sweetie. Take all the time you need."

CHAPTER SIXTEEN

"I NEED to go home."

Rafferty was just on the verge of falling asleep when Elise spoke. She forced her eyes open and her brain caught up a few seconds later. She shifted her weight away and tugged at the blankets, not sure how they might have gotten tangled around them in the few minutes they'd been laying still.

"Okay," Rafferty said, still a bit brain-fogged. "Are you... is everything okay?"

"No, no, wait, not right now," Elise said, pulling Rafferty back down. "I didn't mean right now. I'm sorry. I didn't mean I wanted to leave. Everything's fine."

Rafferty could focus on the world now. She settled against Elise's side and tried to read her face. "Then what did you mean?"

"I need to go *home*-home. To Saratoga Springs."

"Okay." She wasn't used to cuddling against someone. Usually she was the one being cuddled, and she liked the way Elise's arm felt around her. She rested her head on the slope of Elise's chest and allowed herself to be held. "I thought you took care of things last time."

"I did. Sort of." She sighed. "But the more I think about it, the more it feels like I did it... I don't know. Wrong. I snuck up there. I did my best to be seen by the fewest people. I was really only there to get money and, as soon as I got it, I ran away again. I did end things with Michael, but it wasn't authentic. It wasn't right."

Rafferty brushed her hand across Elise's stomach. "So what's the right way?"

"I'm not sure. But it has to be more honest. I don't want to be hiding here. I don't want to worry about someone finding out where I live or work and using it like a weapon. That's the real last step of running away, right? You either have to go back or stand your ground. I like the life I have here. I'm standing my ground."

"Good for you." She lifted up and kissed Elise's lips. "I'm proud of you."

"Thank you."

"Do you want me to come with you?"

Elise raised her eyebrows. "Oh. I hadn't considered that. I think that would be lovely. I wouldn't ask you to do it if it would make you uncomfortable, but I'd like to have you there. However it goes, it's a really long drive back from there."

Rafferty said, "I'll be there."

"Thank you." Elise sat up and kissed her. "Thank you for everything, Rafferty."

"You're welcome. Are you scared?"

Elise sighed and shook her head. "I don't know. One reason I ran away is because I couldn't even bring myself to say the words. It was all theoretical. What I thought I felt, what I thought I wanted. It'll be easier now that I know for sure." She kissed Rafferty's hair. "You were exactly what I was looking for. And I'm so lucky I found you."

Rafferty leaned back and pushed herself up on an elbow. "I appreciate what you're saying, but don't give me so much credit. If you hadn't gotten a job at Achilles, you would have found somewhere else. You would've met someone else, and she would've been the one to confirm what you knew was true before you ever set foot in Manhattan. Now... would she have been as hot as I am? Or as good at sex? Of course not. You *did* get lucky on that count."

Elise laughed.

"But you get the credit for finding yourself. You took the leap without knowing if there was a net, or even ground, down below. I'm just selfishly enjoying the benefits."

"You're so sweet," Elise said. "But I don't know if I would've been as brave with anyone else. You're beautiful, Raff. And you looked so cool in your button-down shirt and suspenders and your red hair tucked up under your cap. And when I saw you roll into the garage, your arm cocked on the window of your cab, looking cooler than Vinnie Barbarino..."

Rafferty grinned. "I'll take that. Hell, I'll even roleplay it if you want."

"Oh... oh, really...?"

She affected a thick Brooklyn accent. "You just say the word, sweetheart." She leaned in and kissed Elise's lips. "And you let me know when you plan to go home. I'll be ready."

"I'm thinking... uh, Thursday."

"Why~" She realized the date. "Oh. Thanksgiving? Is that a good idea?"

Elise shrugged. "I think I'll be more likely to follow through if it's an event day. If it's just, like, a normal Saturday or something, I'd find some reason or another to chicken out. Do it on a holiday. Then there's a solid deadline and no reason to back out."

"As long as it makes sense to you, sweetie."

"I think it makes enough sense to make me go. And if you change your mind about going, I'll understand. But for right now, I'm really happy to have you with me. It'll make it all so much easier."

"I wouldn't miss it for the world." She rubbed her hand over Elise's shoulder. "But for now I would like to go to sleep, if you're done musing."

Elise laughed and kissed her forehead. "Yes, sweetie. I'm sorry. I'm tired, too. We can work out the details when we get up."

"Sounds like a plan."

"And then maybe we'll talk more about your Barbarino roleplay..."

Rafferty, eyes closed, grinned and put her head down on Elise's chest again.

The next night, while they were washing dishes from their dinner, Rafferty stopped so she could put her hair up in a bun. "I wish I could get a haircut before we do the whole Thanksgiving thing."

Elise looked up at Rafferty's hair. "Why? I think it's really nice this long."

"I just like it a little shorter. It feels shaggy when it gets past my shoulders." She rejoined Elise at the sink. "I'm not going to the trouble of taking the subway and going all the way to the shop on one leg. I'll just wear it up. It's no big deal."

"Well, if you want, I could cut it for you."

"You know how to cut hair?"

Elise shrugged. "Sure. I used to cut Mom and Michael's hair all the time. I even cut my own hair." She reached up and flipped her ponytail. "I like it. I find it relaxing. I'd be happy to give you a trim or whatever you need."

"That would be great. Thanks."

"After we finish here?"

"Uh, sure, if that works for you." She smiled and shook her head. "I don't know why I find that so impressive."

Elise blushed. "I can also groom a horse in no time flat."

"Well, I just need you to do my hair. Leave my tail alone."

"No," Elise said, turning to swat Rafferty on the butt. She immediately regretted it, even though Rafferty laughed. "Sorry."

"Don't be sorry. It was the right response." She leaned in and kissed the corner of Elise's mouth. "You can spank me any time you want. Just not at work."

"Obviously."

Rafferty turned back to the sink with a weary sigh. "Work. God. It feels like a thousand years since I was actually at the garage. Has everything changed since I was there?"

"Oh yeah. The cabs fly now."

"Oh, really?"

Elise nodded. "Hovercars, just like in the movies. It's really amazing." She gestured at the window. "I'm surprised you haven't seen them buzz by."

"Oh *that's* what those things are. I thought they were just giant bumblebees."

Elise laughed.

When they finished with the dishes, Rafferty took off her shirt, leaving her in a tank top. She bent over the sink and used the sprayer to wet her hair while Elise laid out newspapers around a chair in the living room. Rafferty joined her and took a seat, then let Elise wrap her in a sheet.

"Did you find a good pair of scissors?"

Elise said, "Yeah, these will do fine. How short did you want it?"

"Anything off the shoulders is fine," Rafferty said. "Just don't cut it short enough you'll have to use clippers. Nothing too butch."

"I think you'd look good butch," Elise said. "Especially in this tank top."

Rafferty said, "Hm. Maybe we'll give it a shot in summer."

Elise rested a hand on Rafferty's shoulder. "You think I'll still be around in summer?"

"Well, I hope you will be." She tilted her head back, looking upside-down at Elise. "I'd like it if you were."

Elise bent down and kissed the tip of her nose. "I won't make you too butch. Now sit up straight. I don't want to make it crooked."

She ran a comb through Rafferty's hair and then, pinching a section between her fingers, began cutting. She hummed while she cut, pausing now and then to check the length.

"Your hair is really beautiful," she said.

"Thanks. I always hated it growing up. Redheads, you know. We don't have it easy."

Elise clicked her tongue. "Kids are dumb. They probably made fun of your freckles, too."

"Oh, god yeah."

"See? Idiots." She brushed the back of her hand over Rafferty's neck. She smiled when it made Rafferty shiver. "I think we're almost there. Just a little more around the ears."

"Sounds good. I forgot to ask how much you charge for a cut."

Elise attempted a thick French accent. "Oh, I am very expensive. My salon caters to the super rich elites. And if you cannot pay, then I will have to make you work off your debt."

"Well, I hate to admit it, but I think I just realized I forgot my wallet."

Elise clicked her tongue again. She grabbed a handful of Rafferty's hair and pulled her head back. Rafferty gasped and went stiff, and Elise immediately let her go.

"Sorry, sorry," she said, dropping the accent. "Are you okay?"

"Yeah," Rafferty said. "Just didn't expect that." She twisted to look up at Elise with a half-smile. "Spanking and now hair-pulling...? You're in some kind of mood tonight."

Elise tucked her hair behind her ears. "Sorry. I-I don't usually... I'm not usually into that sort of thing."

Rafferty faced forward. "Well, if you ever want to explore it..."

"Really?"

"Oh yeah. Didn't like the surprise. But didn't hate the hair-pull."

Elise bent down and kissed Rafferty's hair, then smoothed

down the part she had pulled. "Thank you. I really feel like I'm safe with you. Like no matter what I might be curious about, you'd be willing to let me explore it."

"Sure, Elise. There's a big world out there. Some of it, you're going to want to try out just to see if it fits. And I'm definitely having a good time being your guinea pig. So, yeah, anything you want to explore, you just let me know and I'll pencil you in."

"I will."

There was a knock on the door. Rafferty glanced back to make sure Elise was finished, then reached up to untie the sheet.

"Who is it?"

"Tim!"

Rafferty retrieved her crutches and went to the door. Tim was dressed the same way he always was, thick wool sweater over a plaid button-down, and he was plastic container of cupcakes covered with stickers. He smiled when she opened the door.

"Hey-hey, there she is! How are you doing, kid? You all right?"

"Uh, yeah. I'm fine." She glanced over her shoulder. Elise was cleaning up the newspaper. "What are you doing here?"

He shrugged. "Well, we've been talking about coming to check up on you. Let you know we're thinking about you, all that. But I thought it would be a pain in the butt if we all just showed up and mobbed you. So they elected me. We all chipped in to buy you cupcakes. And, oh... here." He gave her the plastic box to free up his hands. He reached into his back pocket and retrieved a card. "We all signed this. Get Well Soon, you know, the basics."

"Thank you, Tim. This is really sweet of you."

"Sure, you know, we're a bunch of crabby, disgusting assholes, but we do think you're pretty swell. And we all think it sucks how they're treating you. It's hard not to think, you know, could've been any one of us. I know *I* would be screwed if I had to go two months without a paycheck. So if you need anything, anything at all, we're~"

Elise dropped the scissors.

Tim raised his eyebrows and leaned to one side, trying to peek around Rafferty. "You... have guests...?"

"No," Rafferty said.

He narrowed his eyes. "It's the mechanic, isn't it?"

"No," Rafferty said.

"Hi, Elise!"

Rafferty sighed and looked over her shoulder. Elise shrugged and mouthed an apology. When Rafferty looked at Tim again, he was smiling.

"She's just checking in on me," Rafferty said. "Running errands. Cleaning up. Typical coworker shit, you know? Being a friend."

"Oh yeah. Sure. I mean, I figured she was over here a lot. She gives us all so many updates on how you're doing, she'd have to be over here almost every day. Maybe even spending the night."

"You're dangerously close to 'dirty old man' territory, you know that?"

He held up his hands in surrender. "I'm just saying! Not even saying. Barely implying." He looked down, and Rafferty realized she was in a tank top and pajama pants. "Mighty casual dress code for having a coworker over, though."

"Damn it." Rafferty thought about ducking behind the door to grab something to cover up with, but the damage was done. "She was just giving me a haircut."

"That makes sense," he said. "Plausible."

"Truth."

"Uh-huh."

He was still smirking. Despite herself, Rafferty couldn't stop her own smile from starting to break free. When he saw it, Tim chuckled and nodded.

"Okey-dokey. I'll leave you in good hands. Oh, and if you don't already have plans for Thanksgiving, the other drivers are having a potluck at the garage if you want to swing by and see everyone."

"We just... uh, the... we're... I have plans."

He cocked his head to the side. "Yeah? With who?"

Rafferty glared at him.

He grinned like the Cheshire cat. "What are y'all doing?"

"We're going to her parents' place."

Tim laughed and clapped his hands. "Sure. Okay. I've gotta get going. I have some other typical coworker shit I've got to do. Frank and I are going to look at cottages upstate."

"You're a bastard, Tim Kuberski."

He laughed again and turned his back, strolling away down the hall.

Rafferty closed the door. She had to give up one of her crutches to hold the cupcakes, placing them on the table before she went to the kitchen. Elise had just thrown away the newspapers with the hair clippings.

"I didn't mean any of that," Rafferty said.

"Hm?"

"When I told him that you being here didn't mean anything."

Elise furrowed her brow. "Oh." She swept her hair back from her face. "Yeah, sweetie. I knew that."

"I know. I just wanted to be sure I said it." She flexed her grip on her crutch. "You being here means the world to me, Elise. I don't know how I would've gotten through this month without you. And I don't mean the cash, I just mean... I think that..." She looked down at the floor, suddenly very interested in the tile.

Elise went to Rafferty and hugged her. Rafferty leaned against Elise instead of her crutch, still balanced on her good leg.

"I really care about you," Rafferty said. "A lot."

"I know."

"And I want you to keep coming around even after my ankle heals."

Elise laughed. "I will."

Rafferty leaned back. "Promise?"

"Yeah. Promise."

"Because if I have to smash the other ankle to trap you—"

Elise laughed. "I don't think that will be necessary. I'll be here." She kissed Rafferty's cheek, then her lips. "Try to keep me away."

"Good." She rested her forehead against Elise's. "Come into the living room. Tim gave me cupcakes that looked delicious."

Elise said, "Amazing. I love cupcakes." She slipped her arm around Rafferty's waist. "Here, you can give the crutch a rest. Lean on me."

"Are you sure?"

"Yeah, let's go."

Rafferty put her arm around Elise's waist and, together, they made their way back into the living room where she'd left the cupcakes.

CHAPTER SEVENTEEN

THEIR NOCTURNAL schedule made it easy for Rafferty and Elise to be ready before dawn on Thanksgiving morning. They briefly debated whether they needed to bring food, and if they needed to get dressed up. Elise said no to being dressed up - "As long as we're presentable, it'll be fine, we're not fancy." - and they both decided that any food they could provide wouldn't survive a three-hour drive in the car. They set out just as the sun was beginning to color the sky over Central Park.

"Are you nervous?" Rafferty asked as they crossed the George Washington Bridge.

Elise took a deep breath as she considered the question. She drummed her thumbs on the steering wheel and then finally shook her head.

"I'm anxious, I guess? But I think nervous would have more 'scared' in it. I'm not scared. I know there's only one real outcome to today. I say what I'm going to say, then I go home. The only difference is how I interact with my family after this. So no, I wouldn't say I'm nervous."

"That's a lot of words to imply you're calm."

Elise smiled. "Okay. I'm not the most relaxed I've ever been. But I know I'm in the right. I know what I want, and where I want to be. How my mother reacts doesn't matter. It might be uncomfortable, but I know I won't back down." She reached down and took Rafferty's hand. "Besides, I'll have a person there who is in my corner. So what is there to be afraid of?"

"Exactly." She squeezed Elise's hand. "Just say the word if you need me to whack anyone with my crutch. It'll be nice to make it useful."

"You got it."

They drove on in silence for a while before Elise spoke again.

"There *is* something I'm nervous about," she confessed. "I'm nervous about you meeting them. Seeing where I came from. I know you won't judge me, but at the same time... I worry you'll look at me differently."

"We all come from somewhere," Rafferty said. "I'm not going to hold anything I see against you. I've see too much of who you are now to worry about who you might've been before we met. Besides, you left for a reason."

"Right," Elise said.

"It'll be fine."

"I know. I trust you. But feelings are feelings, right?"

"I definitely understand that." She brought Elise's hand up to her lips and kissed the knuckles. "It will be okay."

Elise nodded. "Okay."

"Was there a reason you landed in Manhattan?"

"Because it would be easy to get lost there. Just blend into the crowd. Plus Vic was there, and it was nice to have at least one person I knew nearby. I knew he'd keep quiet if I asked. He was safe. So even though Manhattan was one of the scarier options, he made it feel like the safest at the same time."

"I'm just grateful you wound up making all the choices you made," Rafferty said. "That neighborhood, applying at Achilles, choosing the night shift. So many ways we might never have met."

"You know, I thought about getting a job at a regular garage."

"What made you decide on cabs?"

Elise shrugged. "I don't know. It seemed more steady. I liked the idea of getting to know the people driving the cars instead of just an endless stream of strangers."

Rafferty said, "Can't underestimate friendships."

"Mm-hmm. I can't imagine my life without Bob Groom."

Rafferty laughed. "No matter how hard you try."

They listened to the radio for the rest of the drive, suffering through weak signals that faded into static when they got too far away from the source. Rafferty had an eight-track player and a few tapes that they listened to when the static started to become more prevalent.

It was mid-morning when they arrived in Saratoga Springs. Elise stopped singing along with the tape and sat up straighter in the seat. Rafferty noticed and reached over, resting a hand on Elise's thigh.

When they arrived at the ranch, Elise couldn't help looking at it through Rafferty's eyes. The fence, the fancy gate currently standing open to receive their guests, the majestic house at the end of the long drive. The house was mostly blocked from sight by tall oak trees that had changed various shades of gold, orange, and red but still hadn't started falling. The pasture was empty, but the green grass was perfectly manicured and sparkled with beads of water, either dew or residue from the sprinklers.

Four cars were parked in front of the house. Elise parked behind one of them and settled back into the seat.

"Well. We're here."

Rafferty had been staring at the grounds from the moment they pulled through the gates. Now she turned to look at Elise.

"This is your house? You lived *here?*"

"Yeah. Yep."

"And you traded it for Manhattan?"

Elise looked at Rafferty. The morning sun caught her hair, turning the red into a shining gold. She reached out and brushed the back of her fingers over Rafferty's cheek.

"I traded it for you. No regrets."

Rafferty's eyes flashed with emotion, and she turned away. After she took a moment to compose herself, she sniffed, cleared her throat, and unfastened her seatbelt.

"Are we ready?"

"As we'll ever be," Elise said.

It took Rafferty a moment to get her crutches under her when she got out of the car. Elise waited, then led the way to the wrap-around porch. The kitchen door was standing open, as Elise knew it would be, and she could hear her mother speaking at a very loud - but "not shouting!" - voice at the caterers she'd hired to make sure the day went perfectly.

Elise stopped at the threshold. If Rafferty hadn't been behind her, she knew there was a very real chance she would have turned and ran. She took strength from her and stepped inside.

Ruth was explaining something about mashed potatoes to a woman who looked to be on the verge of quitting entirely. The woman looked at Elise, and Ruth turned to see what had gotten her attention.

"Hi, mom. Happy Thanksgiving."

Ruth's eyes widened. She turned away from the cook, who took the opportunity to flee. "Lisey! Well! Look at you. Beautiful, as always." She smiled brightly and stepped closer. "I wish you would've called. We would have made sure to get your favorites. I think we have everything anyway. Yams, you like yams, right? And pumpkin pie! We definitely have~"

"It's okay, Mom," Elise said. "I'm just~"

"Michael!" Ruth turned at the waist, leaning toward the door that led into the dining room. "Michael, come in here!"

Elise grunted quietly. "Oh no... he doesn't have to..."

Michael came in. He looked at Ruth first, then saw Elise and stopped short. "You're back."

"Before we get *too* carried away," Elise said, "there's something I need to say. I'm not staying. I'll stay for lunch if I'm invited~"

"Of course you're invited," Ruth said, "you're family, why wouldn't you be invited? I know this has been a tough year. But obviously you've come to your senses~"

Elise said, "Mom! Stop. I'm not crawling back. I'm not *back*. I'm here because I'm done running away. I live in Manhattan now. I'm a mechanic for a cab company called Achilles. I have a shitty little apartment, but it's mine. And it's full of second-hand furniture that I chose for myself. And every other week, I take a bag of laundry down the street to wash it at a laundromat." She smiled. "And I'm happy. The only thing I don't like about it is how afraid I am that you'll find out and come drag me away. So I'm telling you now. My life is there now. And I'm not giving up everything I've built just to retreat back here."

Ruth blinked three times, then turned to look at Michael. Her arms were crossed over her chest, and her shoulders were raised as if she was bracing for an attack.

"None of this makes any sense to me," Ruth said when she looked at Elise again.

"It doesn't have to make sense to you," Elise said. "It makes sense to me. I spent my whole life here pretending to be someone I wasn't. Trying to fit into a life that wasn't for me. And yeah, what I'm doing now is harder. And I go to bed completely exhausted some nights. But I'm proud of what I'm doing. And who I am. And *where* I am. I never feel like I'm just going through the motions. I know I'm not following a game plan that someone else wrote for me, and it feels freeing. And it feels right."

Michael pointed at Rafferty. "Who is she?"

Ruth leaned to one side, looking past Elise as if she'd only just realized someone else was in the room with them. Her brow wrinkled.

"Yes, Elise, who is that?"

"This is Sally Rafferty," Elise said. "My girlfriend."

"Oh *honestly*," Ruth snapped, turning away and flipping her hands in the air.

Michael's eyes widened, his eyebrows raised. "Girlfriend?"

Ruth said, "You are completely out of bounds, young lady. I don't know how long you intend to drag this farce out, but this is too far." She looked at Michael. "You must have said something, or had a fight, or~"

"He didn't do anything," Elise snapped. "This is all about me. If I was a different person, Michael would have been a wonderful partner." She looked at him and hoped he could read the apology in her eyes. "You didn't do anything wrong, Michael."

He nodded slowly, but he was still focused on Rafferty.

Ruth said, "Well, she is certainly not welcome here. Taylor and Kimberly are here. Can you imagine what they would think?"

Elise laughed. "I've gone my entire life not giving a shit what Taylor and Kimberly think, and I'm not going to start now."

"And the language! Absolute filth."

"I've said a lot fucking worse, too," Elise said, unable to stop herself. Her face was hot. "And if Sally isn't welcome at your table, then neither am I. I didn't come here for lunch anyway. I just came to tell you I'm not running anymore. I'm not hiding. I'm just going to live my life. I came here to see if that included you." She took a breath and let it out slowly. "And I have my answer."

"Have it your way, then!"

Ruth stepped around Michael and went into the dining room. Elise knew from a lifetime of similar storm-outs that she was probably going upstairs to lock herself in the bedroom for an hour or so. At least the caterers would have a little peace.

Elise turned to Rafferty and nodded at the door. "All right. Let's go."

"We're really just going to leave?" Rafferty whispered. "You're not going to try talking to her or anything?"

"I just tried talking to her," Elise said. "Trust me, it doesn't get better the longer you let her carry on. I've spent a lifetime with that woman and I know when to step away from the table."

Rafferty kept her voice low. "I respect that. But you said the whole reason for this trip was so you could leave the right way. I don't know your mother, or your relationship with her, but this doesn't feel right to me. If you want to go, then I'll go right now. I just want to be sure you won't regret this when we get home."

Elise looked over her shoulder. At some point, Michael had vanished. They were standing alone in the little alcove next to the fridge, in front of the open porch door. It would be so easy to just go back outside, get in the car, and drive back to Manhattan as fast as Rafferty's car could go. But she knew Rafferty was right. If she left now, like this, it would just force her to come back and try a third time.

"Do you mind waiting down here?"

Rafferty smiled. "Not at all." She reached out and took Elise's hand. "Good luck."

"I'm going to need it."

Once Elise went upstairs, Rafferty went back outside. There was a porch swing hanging nearby, and it seemed like the perfect place to get the weight off her leg. She settled onto the seat, propped her crutches against the wall, and used her good foot to start a slow rhythm. The chains gave a comforting creak as she looked out over the stables. She could see horses moving around in the darkness and couldn't help but snicker and shake her head.

"Horses in her backyard. The backyard of her *house*. Horses. Unbelievable."

"Do you want to go say hi to them?"

She looked toward the kitchen door, where Michael awkwardly lurked. He was holding a plate in one hand, a glass of iced tea in the other.

"Maybe before we go," Rafferty said.

Michael ventured out. He was moving like a cat, gauging her approval with every step. When she looked at him again, he lifted the plate like a peace offering.

"Lisey said you didn't come for lunch, but if you really came from Manhattan, that's a long drive. You might as well get something to eat."

Rafferty hesitated, but then she reached out to take the plate. "Thanks. I appreciate that." She nodded at the seat next to her. "Join me?"

"Better than going back in there," he said, taking a seat next to her. His legs were longer, so he was able to take over the swinging just by planting his feet on the porch. Rafferty decided not to fight him and focused on the food. Ham, yams, stuffing, mashed potatoes, green beans, and carrot coins.

"The turkey wasn't quite done yet," he explained.

"That's fine. I'm not a big turkey fan anyway."

He nodded. "Ah. Okay."

She ate her peace offering. He used his feet to swing the seat, watching the stables. She focused on her food so she didn't have to think about him, or what he might be thinking about her.

"So..." He let the word trail off. After a minute he pointed down at her cast. "What happened?"

"Drunk driver smashed into my cab."

He hissed through his teeth. "Ouch."

"It could've been worse. I should get the cast off in about two weeks."

"Mm. Well, that's good."

"Mm-hmm."

He looked at her again, suddenly. "That's why she needed the money, isn't it?"

Rafferty tensed, prepared to defend herself from gold-digger accusations. "I didn't ask her for it."

Michael laughed and shook his head. "No. It's Lisey. You wouldn't have had to ask."

The chains creaked as he continued swinging. She ate some of her mashed potatoes. They had lumps and white gravy, and they were delicious.

"Do you make her happy?"

She looked at him. She hadn't expected that question. There was tension around his eyes, like he didn't want the answer to be 'yes,' but he also couldn't bear if it was 'no.' She rested the plate on her lap and carefully considered her answer.

"I've known Elise for a while now. And I quickly decided I was going to do everything in my power to make her happy, no matter what it took. I know how I would feel if I fell short. I know how much it would hurt if she decided I couldn't give her what she needs. I understand how you feel. So I want you to know I'm not bragging or... or trying to rub your face in it. I just want you to know that yes. Elise is happy with me. And I'm happy with her, too."

He was looking down at his hands. When she stopped talking, he nodded. "That's good. I mean, I hate it. I'm shattered right now. But I've known this was coming for months. I knew as soon as she left that she probably wasn't going to come back. Someone like her... when she leaves... you don't get a second chance. So I'll get over it. As long as she's happy."

Rafferty looked at him again, trying to spot any deception in his expression. "Are you *really* this much of a good guy?"

He laughed and rubbed the bridge of his nose. "Trust me, there's a little lizard part of my brain that wants to scream and break things. But what good would that do? It wouldn't bring her back. It wouldn't change her mind. I'm sad. Anyone losing someone like Lisey... Elise... would feel sad. But I'll get through it."

"That's very mature of you."

Michael said, "But if you're ever beating me at Monopoly, I *will* flip the board."

Rafferty laughed.

He sighed. "And I want to say I never thought she'd end up with a woman," he added, "but that feels wrong to me. When she said 'girlfriend,' it was like... it was like..." He narrowed his eyes and pressed his hands together, struggling to find the right words. "Like someone told you the answer to a riddle you couldn't figure out. And you snap your fingers and say 'oh right, of course, how did I not get that?'"

"Honestly, I think she felt the same way," Rafferty said. "She was very confused for a long time when she first got to New York. She ran away because she couldn't say it out loud until she knew for sure. But she also didn't want to lie to you. Even if it was just a lie of omission."

He smiled ruefully. "Sounds like Lisey." He grunted and rubbed a hand over his face. "God, this sucks. I hate being the good guy and being understanding. Part of me thinks it would feel so much better to knock that plate off your lap and scream in your face."

"I hope you don't," Rafferty said. "The mashed potatoes are really good."

Michael grinned. "I made those."

"Lumps," she said. "I approve."

"Ruth and Lisey insist on smooth," he said with real grief.

"They don't understand. Mashed potatoes needs lumps." He looked at her with a sad smile. "I guess it makes sense we'd have the same taste, huh?"

"I guess so."

"Yeah." He sighed. "Well. Just so you know, if you ever make mashed potatoes for her. She likes it smooth with no lumps."

"It's making me rethink everything."

Michael laughed. "Oh god, it sucks that I kind of like you."

Rafferty smiled. "It's okay. I get it." She looked past him to the door. "How long do you think it'll take them?"

"God knows," he said. "Go ahead and eat. If Lisey hasn't shown up by then, I'll take you out to meet SweetKnight. That's Lisey's horse."

"She has her own horse...?!"

Michael laughed.

Passing through the living room, Elise felt like she had slipped into the Twilight Zone. She half expected Rod Serling to step out from behind the bookcase to give a monologue about her choices. People she hadn't seen since the last holidays all turned cheerful faces toward her. "Oh, it's Lisey! Honey, Lisey is here after all! How have you been, Lisey?" Just hearing their voices made her feel like all the growth she'd achieved in New York had evaporated, leaving her the same sleepwalking mannequin she'd been before she left. It felt like every second she spent in the house would lock her in tighter and tighter until she wouldn't be able to leave. But this was something she had to do.

She muttered quick hellos and "I'm fine, I just need to find my mother" to anyone who spoke to her and hurried through to the hall, then up the stairs.

Her bedroom was just to the right off the landing, and she took a second to peek inside. The same room she'd had growing up, the same room she shared with Michael. The room had grown up with her, and it was an adult's room rather than a child's, but she couldn't help but wonder how much she'd been stunted by seeing the same view out the same window for so long. Her apartment might look out on an alley and a dirty brick wall, but at least it was new.

Elise moved on down the hall. The door to the master bedroom was open and the light was on. She pushed the door open a bit further. Her mother was sitting on the bed, her back to the door. Elise hesitated to step inside - the child version of her once again taking over, insisting she wasn't allowed in her parents' room - but she fought through the block and went in.

"I'm not going to defend my life to you," she said. "I'm not going to try convincing you that I'm right, or that I'm happy. I hope you know that I *am* happy. It's not easy. Some days it's really hard, actually. But I get through those hard days on my own and it makes me feel like I'm accomplishing things. Even if it's just fixing a leaky sink. And Ra- Sally..."

"Yes," her mother snapped without turning around. "What about *Sally?*"

Elise took a moment to steady her breathing so she wouldn't sound angry or defensive when she replied. She thought about swapping books with Rafferty at the laundromat. She thought about the sex shop, and how Rafferty had pushed Elise to take a risk but also respected her boundaries.

"Sally is my safe place," she said.

"Then be her *friend*," Ruth said. "You're not gay."

"Yes," Elise said. "I am. Staying here and marrying Michael wouldn't have changed that. It would have just made me miserable for the rest of my life. I'm glad I left. I'm glad I found someone who is scary and safe at the same time. And she needs me. Not just because of her leg, because I can take care of her. And together we... we work in a way that Michael and I just never did."

Ruth sighed. "I don't know why you're doing this. You had a good life here."

Elise nodded. "I did. I had a great life. I was comfortable here. But it wasn't mine. I need to find a life of my own."

Ruth stood up. She finally turned to face Elise, smoothing her hands over her slacks. "So. What do you want from me?"

"Nothing," Elise said. "Maybe the bare minimum of family support. But if you can't even muster that much, then I guess I don't need anything from you."

"You're more than welcome to stay for lunch," Ruth said, her voice flat. "But that woman isn't welcome here."

"Sally."

"I am not explaining her to our family. To my friends."

Elise shrugged. "It's a simple explanation."

"You can stay," Ruth said again. "She can't."

"Goodbye, Mother."

Elise turned and walked out of the bedroom. She was halfway

down the stairs before her tears threatened, and she stopped to compose herself before she continued. The same people in the living room tried to get her attention again, but they didn't even register to her. She didn't see Rafferty in the kitchen, so she assumed she would be found out on the porch. She didn't anticipate finding her on the porch swing, halfway through a plate of food, laughing with Michael. They looked up as she appeared, their smiles fading when they saw her expression.

"What happened?" Rafferty asked.

Elise shook her head. "It doesn't matter. What... what's happening here?"

Michael stood up. "I got her some lunch. You two have had a long drive. Give me a minute and I'll make one for you, too."

"No, we're not staying."

He didn't stop. "I'll make it to go. You need to eat." Before he stepped around her, he put a hand on her arm and squeezed gently. He leaned in and spoke softly. "I'm not *happy* about this. I wish things were different. But I know getting angry won't change anything, and it'll just make me miserable. So I'm going to try to just be happy that you're happy."

"Thank you," she said.

He looked back at Rafferty, then lowered his voice further. "I don't like that I like her."

Elise laughed and squeezed his arm. "She gets under your skin, doesn't she."

Michael sighed and stepped back. "I'll go get your food. Be right back."

He went into the house and Elise took his seat on the swing. Rafferty put her arm around Elise and guided her head down to rest on her shoulder.

"Are you going to be okay?"

"Yeah," Elise said. "It's sad. But I did my part. I didn't run away. Any distance between us, it's because of her. It hurts."

Rafferty kissed Elise's hair. "I know, sweetie. But I'm proud of you."

"Thank you."

Rafferty speared a carrot coin with her fork and brought it up, offering it to Elise. She plucked it off the fork with her teeth and chewed slowly, turning her head to look at the rest of the offerings.

"Did Michael make the mashed potatoes?"

"Mm-hmm. It had lumps."

"Oh god," Elise groaned.

"Delicious," Rafferty insisted.

Elise turned her head and buried her face in Rafferty's shoulder. "I have terrible taste in partners."

Rafferty laughed and kissed Elise's hair again.

CHAPTER EIGHTEEN

RAFFERTY STROLLED down the ramp into the garage and whistled to get everyone's attention. When the drivers at the card table turned to look, she held her arms out to either side and smiled. It was the middle of December, six weeks after her accident, and the doctor had declared her ankle had mended enough to cut the cast off and free her from the crutches.

"You guys have permission to check me out for a limited amount of time, because I am *back*, baby!" She whooped and kicked her left foot out to show off its missing cast.

The men cheered and applauded her, and she took a bow. Despite her crowing, she was being extremely careful with every step. She'd gotten the cast off a few days earlier, and she was terrified she would do something to put her right back on the disabled list. Every curb was a potential threat, and the stairs at her building were enough to give her a panic attack. Elise assured her that panic would fade with time, but for now Rafferty didn't think there was anything wrong with being a little cautious.

She walked up to the cage, where Mick was watching her with a smile. She raised her eyebrows at him and gestured at her foot.

"Do you see?"

"I see," he said. "Clean bill of health?"

Rafferty shrugged. "They didn't want me running any

marathons, but I specifically asked about driving and my doctor said a hundred percent."

"Did you happen to mention the driving would be taking place over a twelve hour shift?"

"He didn't ask for specifics. I can do it. I've been able to do it since Thanksgiving. I took a few test drives in my own car and it went perfectly. Are you *really* going to turn down an extra driver right before the Christmas crush?" She stuck her hand in the passthrough and made grabby fingers. "Give me a set of keys. I don't care which cab."

Mick sighed and took a keyring off the pegboard. He held it out, then pulled it back. "You've been off the road for almost two months. Are you sure you remember how to do this?"

"Green means go, yellow means go faster, red means go while laying on the horn. The five boroughs are Manhattan, Brooklyn, Queens, Narnia, and Jersey. The Bronx is up and the Battery's down." She sang the last one, then snapped her fingers. "Keys, please."

"Okay, but you're only on-call for tonight. Just to ease you back into it."

She wanted to protest, but she decided to choose her battles. "I'll take what I can get."

He dropped the keyring into her open palm. She pulled her hand back before he could change his mind. She turned and presented the keys to the guys, jingling them as she walked over to the card table. "Good to have you back, kiddo," Tim said. "Place wasn't the same without you."

"It was a lot quieter, for one thing," Bob said.

Rafferty pulled out a chair and sat down. "Nice to know you guys care so much." She looked at Frank. "So I heard a guy on the day shift is Irish."

Tim looked at her, while Hugh and Bob looked at each other in confusion. Frank was doing a crossword and didn't seem to have heard her.

"You hear about that, Frank?" she asked, louder. "Some Irish guy on the day shift?"

He looked up. "What? Who's Irish?"

"Didn't catch the name," she said. "I just can't believe they expect me to drive the same cab some Irishman was in all day. Kind of gives me the shudders."

Frank glared at her. "Now hang on a second. *I'm* Irish. Do you have a problem with me, Raff?" He blinked, realizing. "Rafferty... *You're* Irish!"

She returned his stare, ignoring his realization. "I don't have a problem with you at all, Frank. Do you have a problem with *me?* A woman driving a cab? Not that long ago, I couldn't have had this job. Go back a few decades, you would've been going all over town looking for work and seeing shit like 'Irish Need Not Apply,' right? What about Tim? Or Hugh?" She scanned the table, then settled on Frank again. "So I really don't see the difference between *that* shit and having a gay guy working here."

Frank's face flushed red. "That's a completely different..." He tensed and shifted uncomfortably in his chair. He looked down at the crossword, then sat up straighter. "It's not the same thing!"

"Sure it is," she said.

"It's a *choice.*"

"It's not," Rafferty said, "but okay. For the sake of argument. Religion is a choice. Which religions do you have a problem with?"

Frank sighed. "I-I don't... I'm..."

Rafferty said, "I'm not saying you have to go out for drinks with the guy. But he has as much a right to a job as any of us. There was a time in history where everyone at this table would've been on the other side of the slurs and bullshit. The least we can do is spare him the grief, if we can help it. Think you can pull that off, Frank?"

He grumbled and shrugged, hunching over his paper again. "Sure. I guess."

Rafferty nodded. She looked at Tim, who gave her a 'not bad, kid' nod. She smiled proudly and looked down at the keys she'd been given. The diamond-shaped fob said 307. Not the best of the fleet, but a reliable car. She smiled proudly, feeling like a teenager with a new driver's license. She leaned back in her chair and looked at the clock, counting the minutes until the first call came in.

Rafferty rolled slowly down the street, scanning both sidewalks for any sign of the person who had called for a ride. It was almost two-thirty in the morning. The address she'd been given was in Hell's Kitchen, not far from a sleazy stretch of bars and nightclubs. She was currently on a residential street, but most of the porch lights were out and the streetlights at either corner weren't doing much to push back the shadows between each brownstone.

"It'll look real good if you get mugged your first night back, Raff," she muttered under her breath.

She only had forty dollars in the lockbox under the seat. There had been a lot of conversations around the card table about whether it was better to have a lot of money or a little when a robber demanded you hand it over. A lot would hurt. But if it was just a little, the robber might get angry and take it out on the driver.

At the end of the block, she planned to call it a prank and head back to the garage. She'd almost made it when a tall figure peeled away from the shadows between two buildings and stepped into the street. He raised his hand as her headlights illuminated his long dark coat. She swore under her breath and rolled to a stop. She checked her mirrors for potential accomplices as he hurried toward the cab.

He opened the back door and leaned in. "Are you here for Jordan?"

She twisted in the seat to look at him through the partition. "That's right."

"That's me," he said, sliding into the seat.

He pulled the door shut and began fishing for the seatbelt. Now that she could see him under the dome light, she realized he was wearing something bright red underneath his coat. He was also wearing eyeshadow, lipstick, and rouge, but he was missing false eyelashes and his haircut was distinctly male. She wondered if he had a wig hidden in one of the pockets of his jacket.

"Sorry if I scared you," he said. "I like to get a look at the driver picking me up before I get in a car with them."

"That makes sense." Rafferty shuddered to think what might have happened if Frank had been on-call. "We're heading to SoHo?"

"That's right."

She faced forward again and set out. "So. Women drivers are safe?"

"In general," he said. "I would've flagged down a man, too, depending."

"Depending on what?"

"A lot of things. You can just tell if he's going to be more trouble than it's worth. Like, a lot of the older guys, they might not like it, but they'd also be way too uncomfortable to say anything. So it'd be a silent ride. Which isn't a bad thing. You've just gotta hang back and get the vibe of 'em, you know? I mean, I'm sure you know. You've dealt with men before."

"Sure," she said, smiling.

"And some women might be even worse than any men. Oh, some of the things women have screamed at me when I'm just out walking down the street. Good 'Christian' women, huh." He shook his head and looked out the window with a sigh.

"So I passed the test?" Rafferty said.

"Oh, easily. I liked your suspenders."

Rafferty laughed and looked down. "Noted. Suspenders make me trustworthy."

"There was also something about your eyes. You've got kind eyes."

"Well, thank you very much." She looked at him in the rearview. "The name is Jordan?"

"Mm-hmm." He looked at the license displayed on the partition. "Sally Rafferty. It's very nice to meet you, Sally Rafferty."

She nodded. "Same to you."

She headed south on 11th Avenue. At this time of night, it would be a straight shot with very little chance of traffic getting in their way.

"I have a girlfriend."

Jordan had been looking out the window and turned to face her. "Oh, really?"

"Her name is Elise. She's a mechanic at the cab company. That's how we met."

"Huh!" He laughed. "Well, I guess I'm a pretty good judge of character. A cabbie and a mechanic. That's so sweet."

Rafferty smiled at him in the rearview mirror. "It's nice to talk about her. I don't get a lot of opportunities, for obvious reasons."

"We've got time, girl," Jordan said. "Tell me about her."

"Oh, boy. Well. She's kind of naïve. Not in a bad way. She just had a very isolated childhood, and grew up very, uh... very..." She searched for the right word. "Insulated, I guess. She's almost ten years older than me, but I almost always feel like I'm the one with all the experience. And I get to show her things and see her experience them for the first time."

Jordan chuckled softly. "That's beautiful. And what does she do for you?"

"She takes care of me," Rafferty said. "I was hurt a few weeks back. My ankle. I couldn't work. I couldn't walk, because that first day I barely knew how to hold the crutches let alone use them right. So I went home, and I fell on the couch and I..." She gripped the steering wheel harder. "I haven't even told *her* this... but I was thinking some pretty dark thoughts. Not... not, like, actual plans. I wasn't..." She met Jordan's eyes in the mirror. "You know how you can think about something without actually planning to go through with it?"

He nodded sagely. "Oh yes. Yeah."

"Well. I was thinking bad things. I didn't have enough money saved to get me through an extended period of unemployment. And part of me thought that it would be stupid to suffer for no reason. I didn't think I would do anything permanent. But I did lay there and wonder if this was going to be the end. I couldn't see a way back to my real life from that moment.

"Then Elise showed up. And she had answers. And she cooked me dinner, made me get up and act like a person. So I faked it, because I liked her, and I liked being with her, and the more time went by, the less I was faking. There was a light at the end of the tunnel, suddenly, and Elise was there to show me how to get there."

"Have you told her any of that?"

"No," Rafferty said. "But I should. I will."

"Good. People need to know that kind of thing. You never know when it actually *will* be the end, you know? Meteor could fall outta the sky right now and pancake this cab."

Rafferty looked up at the sky. "Or a drunk could slam my ankle into the curb."

"Ouch!" Jordan hissed through his teeth. "Yeah. Or that."

When they reached his destination, she pulled to the curb where he indicated. He glanced at the meter and passed a five dollar bill through the partition.

"Thank you for the ride, Miss Sally."

"You're welcome. And hey, wait. Just a second."

He already had the door open, leaning halfway out of the cab. "You keep the change."

"No... I mean, thank you. But I wanted to give you something." She took an Achilles business card off the sun visor. She wrote her name on the back, then passed it to him. "The next time you need a ride at this time of night, call and ask for me. Even if I'm on the road, the dispatcher can get me on the radio. You can share that with your friends, too."

Jordan took the card. "Thank you, Sally. Can I have a couple more cards?"

"Sure." She took a few more off the stack and handed them over. "You shouldn't have to gamble on whether you'll get a safe ride home at night."

He sniffled and fought through a brief twitch of sincere emotion. Then he nodded. "Thank you."

"Have a good night, Jordan. And merry Christmas."

"Merry Christmas to you. And to your girl, Elise. Treat her right."

She grinned. "Will do."

She waited until he was safely inside the building before she pulled back out onto the road. Mick didn't like it when drivers did that, or when callers specifically requested someone, but she was willing to risk his irritation in this particular case. There were a lot of people like Jordan out there who just needed a safe, reliable way to get home. If she could provide that, she was willing to deal with Mick's irritation at a bent rule.

Being on-call meant that instead of just circling the city looking for another fare, she had to go back to the garage and wait for another call. Normally she didn't mind that, but tonight it felt unfair. She'd missed seeing the nightside of the city. The light from the all-night places, the shuttered businesses that looked like they'd been abandoned decades ago, the people shuffling down the sidewalk on their way to early shifts or home from late shifts. It felt like coming home, and she wasn't looking forward to going back to a dark, quiet garage.

Her mood changed, however, when she pulled in and saw Elise sitting alone at the card table. Elise looked up at the sound of the cab and smiled when she saw who it was. She'd been having lunch and reading, but she closed the book in anticipation of Rafferty joining her. Rafferty parked, thinking about the half-eaten sandwich in Elise's hand. Rafferty had made that for her before work. There was something so simple about it, so casually intimate, that she took a second to sit in the quiet car and let the information sink in.

She finally got out of the cab and went to the card table. Elise smiled up at her and tapped the open bag of chips next to her sandwich.

"Want to share? I got the sour cream ones you like."

"Thank you." Rafferty plucked one out of the bag as she sat down.

"Did everything go okay out there?" Elise asked.

Rafferty nodded. "Perfect. It was so nice to get back out on the road. I should've done this weeks ago."

"You couldn't have done it weeks ago. You needed to heal. I

might not agree with the company throwing you out into the cold, but I'm glad you didn't try to work with your ankle all banged up."

"It was my left foot," Rafferty sighed.

Elise said, "It doesn't matter! It would have been reckless."

Rafferty sighed.

"I know, I know, I'm being a nag."

"Yeah." Raffety lightly bumped Elise's foot under the table. "But it's nice to have someone who cares enough to nag."

Elise smiled at her. "Well, keep making boneheaded decisions and I'll keep nagging."

"I think I can make that deal."

Watching Elise, Rafferty was suddenly overcome. Just watching her sit and pick the crust off her sandwich and pop it into her mouth...

"I..."

Elise looked up at her, still chewing. Rafferty felt like a deer in the headlights looking into them. Bright blue eyes like lasers, locking her in place. She desperately wanted to say the words caught in her throat, but she didn't want to say them here, at work, out of nowhere. She didn't want to whisper it and hope no one overheard. The words she wanted to say deserved to be said at full voice, with no hesitation or concern. She'd already ruined that by stopping mid-sentence, and there was no way to salvage this moment. So instead, she stole another chip.

"I think I'm going to eat all your chips."

Elise grinned and pushed the bag closer to her. "Go nuts."

Rafferty took the bag. Elise opened her book and started reading again. Rafferty watched her. She would say the words she'd held back. She'd say them soon, as soon as possible, but she'd wait for the right moment.

CHAPTER NINETEEN

ELISE WOKE up in Rafferty's bed on the last day of the year. She took a moment every time that happened just to appreciate the reality of it. She was in Sally Rafferty's bed. Despite constant reassurances, the desperate side of her brain had been certain her days in the apartment were numbered. She had briefly, very briefly, worried that her invitations would dwindle once Rafferty got the cast off. Her fears were quickly eased when Rafferty invited her over for dinner as they were leaving the doctor's office. It had been two weeks since that day, and Elise hadn't spent a single night in her own bed.

They'd made love the night before. She smiled at the memory as she stretched and rolled onto her back. Rafferty was still asleep, fist caught between her cheek and pillow, her lips slack. Elise watched her sleep for a minute or two, then slipped out of bed and went to make them breakfast.

A few days earlier, she'd received a letter at Achilles. Mick announced it by shouting, "Herald! Letter!" over the intercom.

Hugh, sitting at the card table, said, "No one here named Harold..."

She glared playfully at him as she passed. "Really, Hugh? Every time?"

"What?" he said, oblivious.

The letter had been from Michael, inviting her to come up for Christmas. She had Mick break a dollar, then used a quarter on the payphone to call him.

"Lisey?" he grumbled into the phone. "Geez, what time is it?"

"Sorry," she said. "Did I mention I work nights at the garage? Anyway, I wanted to see if your invitation was on behalf of *everyone* or just you."

"I've been chipping away at Ruth," he said, his voice slightly more awake by that point. "I think she'll get to acceptance in time. She's just, you know, set in her ways. And a lot of it is being scared, you know? Being gay is kind of dangerous these days."

"As opposed to the past, when it was all sunshine and roses."

"You know what I mean."

She sighed and leaned against the post. She regretted making the call at work, but she needed to know the answer to her question. She had to be careful what she said, in case anyone was eavesdropping.

"Is the invitation just for me?"

Michael hesitated. "I-I think it would be best if it was just you. This time! Just this time. We have to ease her into the idea that you're a different person now."

She smiled sadly. "But I'm not, Michael. *You* understand that, right? I'm the same person you've always known, I'm just... more aware of who that person is. And being that person means not showing up alone."

He sighed. "I... okay. I understand. But if you and Sally want to come up and have Christmas dinner with *me* somewhere, Ruth doesn't have to know. I'd like to get to know her a little better. Make sure she deserves you."

Elise laughed. "Oh, now you're the judge of that?"

"Someone's got to look out for you, Lisey. Is she still on the crutches?"

"No, she got them off a week or so back."

"Good. Good. Okay. Let me know if you're coming up. I'll figure out, uh... there's gotta be a Chinese place around here we can meet up without Ruth sticking her nose in."

"Will do. I'll let you go back to sleep."

"Thanks. Take care of yourself, L... Elise."

She smiled. "Thank you, Michael. For everything. Merry Christmas."

"You too."

Remembering the call had almost caused her to burn the bacon. She transferred it to the plate as Rafferty appeared from the bedroom. She was still wearing her briefs and T-shirt, rubbing her eyes before she pushed her hair out of her face.

"Are you burning down my apartment?" she mumbled.

"Trying not to."

Rafferty embraced her from behind and kissed her neck. "Morning."

"Good morning." She reached back to rest her hand on Rafferty's hip. "I'll have eggs ready in a second."

"I'll pour the OJ."

Rafferty gave Elise another squeeze before she pulled away and went to the fridge.

They had indeed ended up spending Christmas on the road to Saratoga Springs. They had a nice lunch with Michael at a Chinese restaurant, and Elise didn't know if she was thrilled or horrified with how well Rafferty got along with him. It got to the point where she felt like a third wheel on their date. But just as her worry was starting to turn into a real, tangible thing, Rafferty's hand found hers under the table and squeezed. That had been enough to calm her paranoia enough for her to enjoy the meal.

And it was good that they got along. It was good that Michael understood, and he seemed to genuinely support their relationship. It meant she still had ties to home, just in case. She didn't plan to go back any time soon, and definitely not to stay, but it was nice knowing the bridge hadn't been burned.

"We don't have enough OJ for both of us. Would you rather have that or milk?" She held up the offerings. "Or I could put on pants and run down to the store."

"Milk's fine," Elise said. "Please don't put on pants."

Rafferty smiled and poured their glasses. Elise finished cooking and took their plates to the dinner table. Elise was off for the holiday, but Rafferty had volunteered to come in. Her reasoning was that she'd had enough vacation to last a lifetime. She didn't want to give up a night behind the wheel unless she absolutely had to.

"So," Rafferty said, starting to wake up now that she'd eaten, "do you have plans for the day?"

"I have to go home, get some clothes, go do some laundry." She plucked at the borrowed shirt she was wearing. "Not that I mind smelling like you."

Rafferty said, "You can bring some stuff over here if you want. I've got plenty of space."

Elise raised an eyebrow. "Really? Are you..."

"Hm?" Rafferty looked up from her plate.

"Sorry. Are you asking me to move in?"

Rafferty sat up straighter, eyes darting left and then right. She didn't look trapped, she looked like she was analyzing her own words.

"I wouldn't mind," Rafferty said. "I like having you here. Do you want to move in?"

"No," Elise said. "Sorry. I mean I also like being here. But I also like having my own place. I've never had that before. And even if I'm not spending much time there, I like knowing I have the option."

Rafferty nodded. "That makes a lot of sense. I wasn't asking you to move in. Not that I'd be..."

"No, and not that I don't want to."

"Right." She chuckled and shifted in her chair. "That was a little awkward."

Elise shrugged. "Yeah. But only a little." She reached across the table, offering her hand. Rafferty took it. "Neither of us are there. Yet. But we're both open to the possibility."

Rafferty squeezed Elise's fingers. "That's my take away."

"Good." She took her hand back. "So! Uh, yes. Laundry today. And I might take you up on leaving some things here, just to make things more convenient."

"Right. So, if you're free around eleven thirty, quarter to midnight, how about I come pick you up? We can go somewhere and watch the fireworks at midnight."

Elise raised her eyebrows. "Really? I figured you'll be insanely busy tonight."

"Most of the night, sure. Sunset until around eleven is going to be gangbusters. And then probably twelve-thirty to two or three will be just as nuts. But by eleven-thirty on New Year's Eve, most people are already wherever they're planning to be at midnight. So I'm almost positive I'll be free."

Elise grinned and nodded. "Then yes, absolutely! I'll be ready. Where are you taking me? Times Square?"

"*God* no. Only tourists and insane people go there. I know a special place."

"I can't wait."

They finished eating and Rafferty checked her watch. "I need to go get ready. Will you be here when I get out of the shower?"

"No, I'll probably head home."

"Okay. Have a good day." Rafferty stood and bent down to kiss Elise. "See you tonight. Here. Quarter to midnight."

"I'll be here."

She watched Rafferty go down the hall and took a moment to appreciate the moment. In a minute, she was going to get up and wash the breakfast dishes. While Rafferty was in the shower. Then she would do laundry, and they would meet up later. It was so domestic, she had to laugh. When she ran away from the ranch, part of her had wondered if she was just afraid of commitment and becoming a wife. And while she was a far cry from being Rafferty's wife, she was definitely nesting. Chores. Just dirty dishes and doing laundry.

Sometimes being a homemaker wasn't the worst thing in the world, if it was the right home.

Elise was waiting in the lobby of Rafferty's building at eleven thirty. She'd never really taken the time to explore the space. It was lovely, in a sort of grimy and neglected way. Leaves that had blown in around people's feet had accumulated in the corner by the stairwell, and the tile hadn't been scrubbed in ages. The windows looking out over the sidewalk were clean enough, but so much grime had gathered around the edges that meant only the center of each pane served as a functional window.

She knew it was only a matter of time before she was annoyed by these things. She knew one day she'd come in and wrinkle her nose at the mess, or there would be a fast-food bag tumbled in among the leaves. But for the time being, it showed the building was a place where actual people lived.

It was just before 11:46 when Rafferty pulled up in front of the building. Elise smiled and stepped outside, huddled against the cold as she jogged down the walkway and ducked into the backseat.

Rafferty twisted to look at her through the partition. "You can sit up here if you want."

"I want the full taxi experience," Elise said.

"Ahh, okay. Well, then." She tugged on the brim of her cap and faced forward. "Where ya headin', miss?"

Elise grinned. "I'm heading out to meet my girlfriend at... ah, she just said it was a special place."

"Ah yeah, I know where that is. I can get you there, no problem." She pulled away from the curb. "So, having a good night?"

"Pretty good," Elise said. "Looking forward to the fireworks."

Rafferty nodded. "Yeah, they're always something else." She looked at Elise in the rearview mirror. "So you said you've got a girlfriend, huh?"

Elise laughed. "Yeah."

"Nice, nice. I've got someone, too."

"Oh really? Well, that's wonderful."

"Yeah. Beautiful girl. Older than me, but that's fine. As long as she doesn't worry about robbing the cradle with me."

Elise laughed again. "I'm sure she doesn't think of the age gap very often."

"Here's hoping." She turned her wrist to look at the face of her far-too-big watch. "Oof. You know, there's a chance you're still going to be in this cab at midnight. And you know, midnight on New Year's Eve? I hope your girl isn't the jealous sort. Traditions are traditions."

"Oh, dear. Well, I guess it's my own fault for not going out earlier. You can't fight tradition. I'm sure she'll understand."

Rafferty said, "Well, that's good. I'd hate to overstep."

Elise shook her head, still smiling. "You're such a goofball."

"You think *I'm* bad, you should see the weirdo I'm dating."

Elise kicked the back of the seat, which made Rafferty laugh.

A few minutes later, when Rafferty pulled to the curb and parked, Elise unfastened her seatbelt and excitedly looked out the window. She was confused when she saw trees. On the driver's side of the car, there was only a row of closed shops.

"Where are we?"

"Bryant Park." Rafferty twisted to look at her. "You should move to the front seat now. It'll be much better if you aren't watching through the partition."

"Watching what?" Elise didn't wait for an answer. She got out, opened the front passenger door, and slid in next to Rafferty. "What happens in Bryant Park on New Year's?"

"Nothing." Rafferty took off her watch and draped it over the meter. Two minutes to midnight. "Just watch the sky to the northwest. Above the library. That's where the Times Square fireworks will be going off once the clock strikes midnight. The library and the park create enough open space that you can see enough of the sky to make a good show."

Elise reached for Rafferty's hand. "Thank you for sharing this with me."

"You're welcome." She looked at the watch. "We're getting close now."

"Yeah." She looked at the sky again, then back to the second hand, sweeping around the face. "Are we going to do the countdown or just~"

"I love you."

Elise looked at Rafferty, startled enough that she couldn't find any words.

"I've wanted to say it for a while. I've been holding off, because I wanted the time to be right. And I thought, what better time than the start of a new year, right? So... yeah. I love you."

The first firework exploded, which startled Elise into breaking eye contact. A huge yellow star had appeared in a stretch of sky that had moments ago been completely dark. A green firework exploded behind it, along with a red and a blue. Elise had felt each pop like a blow to the chest. Or maybe her heart was just thundering that hard. She couldn't really tell at the moment.

She looked away from the display. Rafferty was looking at her with a mixture of hope and concern. The fireworks continued, lighting up one side of Rafferty's face while the other half remained in darkness.

"I love you too, Rafferty."

Rafferty let go of the breath she'd been holding. She laughed and shook her head. "That was cruel, Elise."

"No, I-I was just overwhelmed by the~"

"I know," Rafferty said. "I know." She leaned across the seat and cupped Elise's face. "Happy new year, Elise."

"Happy~"

The next two words were smothered by Rafferty's kiss. The kiss continued for almost a full minute, carrying on through the percussive blasts of nearby fireworks.

When they finally parted, Rafferty brushed her thumb over Elise's lips. "New year. Zero hour."

"Zero hour in Zero City," Elise said.

Rafferty laughed. The fireworks were lighting up her eyes like something magical was happening. "Nothing but open road ahead of us."

Elise smiled. "Nothing but possibilities."

She couldn't wait to see what laid ahead.

ABOUT THE AUTHOR

Geonn Cannon is the author of over sixty novels, including the Riley Parra series which was adapted into an Emmy-nominated webseries by Tello Films. His novel *Can You Hear Me* was adapted into *Static Space*, an award-winning short film. He's also written two tie-in novels for the television series *Stargate SG-1*. He was the first male author to win a Golden Crown Literary Society Award for his novel *Gemini*, and he won a second for *Dogs of War*.

www.ingramcontent.com/pod-product-compliance
Lightning Source LLC
Chambersburg PA
CBHW071931190726
48293CB00004B/1236